Joy Again

Molly Krause

Flint Hills Publishing

Cover Design by Amy Albright

stonypointgraphics.weebly.com

Flint Hills Publishing
Topeka, Kansas

www.flinthillspublishing.com

Printed in the U.S.A.

ISBN-13: 978-0-9997547-2-6
ISBN-10: 0-9997547-2-6

Some of you say, "Joy is greater than sorrow,"
and others say, "Nay, sorrow is the greater."
But I say unto you, they are inseparable.
Together they come, and when one sits
alone with you at your board, remember
that the other is asleep upon your bed.

—KAHLIL GIBRAN *THE PROPHET*

.

JOYCE

JOYCE WALKED INTO her office on Friday morning and the first thing she noticed was a box on top of a stack of food service invoices, wrapped in Snoopy gift paper. From her daughter Cassie. It had to be; Snoopy was their inside joke. Joyce had been giving Cassie a card with the famous beagle on it for her birthday for as long as she could remember. But Joyce's birthday wasn't for months—what could this be for?

She walked past boxes of toilet paper, to-go cups, and rubber gloves to fall into her chair. When had her office turned into the supply closet? Andy used to be the one to check in the orders and keep them organized. She needed to talk to Maggie about relabeling the closet to give her some space. Space was all she seemed to want these days.

The box had more weight to it than she expected. She carefully opened the wrap, thinking she could reuse it. A shoebox was revealed. She opened the lid and saw a piece of paper folded on top with "MOM" written in bold handwriting. She unfolded it and saw that it was a registration form for the San Diego Marathon with her name and information filled in the blanks with the same bold handwriting.

Written on a sticky note attached to the form:

Did you see what day it is? Please do it with me!

BTW, this is your early birthday present.

Love you, Cassie

PS - Please!

She leaned back in her chair and closed her eyes. A marathon was the last thing in the world she wanted to do. But Cassie rarely asked her to do anything. She was so independent—had been since she took her first steps out the front door and didn't look back. She hadn't changed much since she was a toddler really, always running, rarely pausing. At twenty-three Cassie had already run two marathons, her dad ran the last one with her a year ago.

Joyce's phone dinged with the sound of a text received.

Mrs. Becker I think I've got the flu. Don't want to pass germs to customers. This is Grace.

Joyce punched in the words she had said or written a thousand times.

It's your responsibility to find a replacement for your shift. Failure to do so will result in a no call/no show write up.

There was no response, nor did she expect one.

She removed one of the shoes from the box. It had a ridiculously thick sole—like a clown shoe almost—and was bright coral. She had to admit that the cushioning looked appealing to her aging joints. She had never liked to run, although she used to force herself to do it a couple of times a week for exercise. The only thing she been forcing herself to do for the last year was to go to work.

Another text dropped in. Thinking it was Grace again giving someone's name as her replacement for her lunch shift, she grabbed her phone. It was Cassie.

SOOO???

Thank you for the shoes, honey. They are…colorful.

Will you?

Let me think about it.

Do you want some polenta with a fried egg?

What? Are you here?

Cassie peeked her blond head around the open doorway. She smiled and walked in, holding two plates in her left hand. With flourish she reached with her right hand to remove two forks from her back pocket.

"Voilà. Your breakfast. I made it myself."

"What a great surprise, thank you." Joyce took the plate and placed it on top of the box. She gazed at Cassie as she got settled into a chair facing her desk and balanced her own plate on her knees. With her hair pulled back into a ponytail, Cassie still looked so young, like she had when she used to come and play restaurant while Joyce and Andy worked.

Joyce dug into one of the boxes on the floor, opened a package of napkins, and handed one to Cassie. She pierced her fork into the egg and the yolk oozed from its center—cooked perfectly. The mound of soft polenta was flecked with scallions, black pepper, and shaved Parmesan cheese. It was a shame she didn't feel hungry; she almost always had to force herself to eat these days.

"This looks great. You know, Maggie might have a job for you in the kitchen if this higher education thing doesn't work out." Joyce ate a forkful. It was delicious. Cassie had learned a lot from her dad.

"Ha, ha. I'll take my chances with law school. But it's nice to know I have something to fall back on." Cassie eagerly ate from her plate, her metabolism and exercise routine allowing her to eat whatever she wanted and still maintain her slim, athletic build.

"I thought classes started this week," Joyce said as she

finished up her food.

"They do, just have orientation this afternoon, no big deal." Cassie shifted uncomfortably in her chair. "I know you want to think about it, but I hope you'll do the marathon with me. It would be good for you. Good for us."

Joyce took in her daughter as she was talking. Cassie really was too good looking for her own good, way better looking than Joyce or Andy, even when they were young. She always thought that only the beautiful traits were selected from their DNA in her creating.

"I know you're doing your yoga at home still, but getting outside is different, it's better. And we can train together. And did you see what the date is?"

Joyce shook her head; she hadn't gotten that far yet.

"Dad's birthday, May thirty-first. Don't you see?"

What she saw was her only child desperately trying to connect with her in the one activity that had always provided satisfaction and pleasure, one in which she had shared with Andy, who could no longer participate. How could she say no?

"Do I have to wear the shoes?" Joyce asked with a smile.

"You will love the shoes, I promise. I researched which

would be best for your joints. Oh, I'm so excited!" Cassie pulled a piece of paper from her pocket and handed it to Joyce. "Here is a sample training schedule I came up for us. We have plenty of time to train for this." She hugged Joyce and whispered, "Thanks, Mom," before she cleared the plates from the desk and ran out the door.

MAGGIE

"I DIDN'T ORDER this." Maggie glared at the disinterested delivery guy and held a plastic bag full of frozen, gray pellets for him to look at. "Is this that meat-like substance? Didn't the FDA outlaw this?"

He didn't lift his head from his electronic hand-held keypad. "Circle it on the sheet, you'll get a credit."

"Hellooo." She got right under his face, waving the bag. "How did this crap get into my kitchen?" He shrugged. "This is what you get when you give your order to a computer. Where are my leeks?"

He pointed at the order sheet. "If it's on the sheet, it's in a box."

She was trying to control her irritation, but the truth was she enjoyed letting it out on occasion. Since taking over for Andy in the kitchen, she found that it was perfectly acceptable to throw temper tantrums on the job. That was a huge change from her almost-decade as a flight attendant. Those shifts were a constant battle of hiding her thoughts from the people around her. Keeping the edge out of her voice when asked for the hundredth time in one day what kind of juice was served. Not snapping when someone protested about putting the tray table up. Ignoring a stray hand that grabbed her ass as she walked by.

"Oh, here they are." She pulled out a large bunch of pale green leeks, browning around the edges. "But they look like shit. I can't use these." She shoved them back in the box and circled them on the sheet.

Maybe she was creating some drama where there wasn't any. She was getting restless and so far had been channeling those feelings into her growing tattoos. Finally liberated from having to hide them while wearing her uniform, she was adding two large cuffs around her biceps. Abstract and colorful, she'd respond, "Jesus, they don't mean anything," when asked what they represented. "They're just pretty, why do they have to have more significance than that?"

Her sister Joyce's response to her changing flesh was, "I think you may be watching too much Food Network. You know, you don't really have to be fully tatted to work in a kitchen."

Because Andy didn't have any, she knew Joyce wanted to say, but didn't.

The menu was overdue for a major change, but Maggie was reluctant to bring it up with Joyce. The Italian-American menu that Andy's Café had served for almost twenty years was in serious need of a facelift. When she saw Toasted Ravioli printed on a ticket, hanging from the wheel on the cooking line, she wanted to scream with frustration. What kind of idiot orders toasted ravioli? Then she remembered she was the idiot *making* toasted ravioli. And don't even get her started on the décor.

Housed in a strip mall in central Tulsa, wedged between a hardware store and an appliance repair shop, Andy's Café had a casual bistro feel when it first opened. Cane-backed chairs, checkered tablecloths, and a long wooden bar with heavy stools. Now it had the energy and vibe of a nursing home—burgundy-patterned carpet in an attempt to hide the wear, artificial flowers in a large vase at the hostess station, elevator music that seemed vaguely familiar. They had plenty of customers, regulars who felt like family, but even in Tulsa, where trends were slow to come and go, Maggie knew the café was gasping its final breaths.

She was waiting for Joyce to come out of her zombie phase and re-enter the living world. Joyce always showed up for work, made the schedule, completed payroll, paid the bills, even talked to customers. But she was like the shell of her older sister, almost pretending to be Joyce, going through the motions out of habit and routine. They had both experienced loss before—their dad was killed in a car crash when they were just kids; their mom suffered horribly from lung cancer before she died five years ago. But what Joyce became after Andy's death worried Maggie.

Even when they were drinking at the bar at the end of a busy night of service, when hardly anyone else was around, Joyce had her mask on. They would laugh together, making fun of their employees (*Did you hear how Kate pronounced linguini? I didn't know you could fit so many syllables in that word*) or customers' requests *(I hate to be the one to tell her, but getting the dressing on the side isn't going to help her get that dress zipped back up)*. It almost seemed normal. But then Joyce would fall silent.

She felt she owed it to Joyce to be the rock in their small family now; Joyce had always been the rock in the past. As their mother was dying, it was Joyce who took her to the many doctor appointments, picked up her prescriptions, arranged for hospice, and finally just sat in a chair next to her bed reading out loud from the newspaper.

Maggie would fly in for a couple of days then beg off, saying she had to return to work. She would never forget what Joyce had said to her as she was leaving from the last visit she made to their mom.

After an awkward pause as Maggie had kissed their unresponsive mom, Joyce looked up from her book and said, "Dying is pretty boring, isn't it?"

DAN

THE FIRST FREE breakfast Dan ate at the extended hotel where he had been living for the past month was confusing. He was convinced the round disk he smothered in syrup was a pancake, but the texture was spongy and chunky as he chewed. Actually some version of scrambled eggs, a closer examination revealed. He switched to packets of oatmeal and the slightly bruised apples that were on the buffet table every morning.

The hotel was sterile and impersonal; he counted the stains on the carpet in the hallway as he walked to his room. He had thought he would only be there a few nights to give Laura a chance to cool off. He had underestimated her anger toward him.

He stayed at the hotel because of its close proximity to the university and the indoor pool. The pool gave him an easy activity when he had evenings and weekends with his sons. With his oldest away at law school, he was left with the three younger boys. He felt a mixture of fury and sorrow when he drove up to his house to pick them up, the home *his* salary had paid for, and honked at the curb because his wife didn't want to see him. He had been such an ass.

But as much as he liked having someone making his bed—Laura could care less about such things—he didn't think he could handle another night going into the parking lot, pulling his Suburban under the bright, fluorescent lights. It was so very quiet in his room as he was preparing for his new class, *Political Shakespeare and Modern Parallels*.

At first he relished the solitude, since his household with four sons was accented by bursts of noise—a basketball dribbled on the wood floor, silverware dropped on the kitchen tile, fighting over the remote control in the living room. It drove him crazy. God, he missed it.

He had to go back home; he was feeling desperate and horny. He hadn't seen Amber since that awful day, his wife wouldn't talk to him much less touch him, and he didn't know how much longer he could keep living this way. Two weeks ago he sent Laura a text that read, "We need to talk." Her reply was, "Talk to what's her name. Amber?" He replied, "I miss you." She didn't reply, which he took as a good sign.

He decided he needed to make a bold move, a grand romantic gesture. It was the only way he could see to regain his life. First, he needed a babysitter, someone to get and keep the boys out of the house for a few hours. He had never scheduled a babysitter in all of his years as a father and was stumped. The only group of people he could think to draw on was his students, and given his current circumstances, that would only make the situation worse. He called Laura's friend, their next-door neighbor, Rhonda.

"Hi, Rhonda, it's Dan. Can I talk to you for a minute, please? I could really use your help."

"Well, I'll be dammed. I've known you for almost fifteen years and never had the pleasure of getting a call from you Dan. To what do I owe the honor?"

"Come on. I know you know what's going on. You know this isn't good for the boys. You and Mike have had your issues too. Please, I just have a question."

"I'm all ears. What is it?" she asked.

"Can you keep the boys for a few hours Friday night? Or know someone who Laura would approve of to do it?"

"Why? What's going on?"

"I want to surprise her, cook dinner for her in the house. We need some time alone together."

Rhonda sighed loudly. "I don't know. She's taking this pretty hard, she may need more time."

"Please. Have I ever asked you for anything?"

Dan rarely asked anyone for anything, actually. If he wanted it, he would just take it—or find a way to make it available to himself. Like most personality traits, the resourcefulness that had brought him so many benefits had also been what caused him so much grief.

"Okay, okay. I'll take them. I'm not going to lie to her though, you work out the details."

It was the first moment of hope for him in over a month. He smiled as walked out of his room, ignoring the carpet stains. Instead of just waiting, he started planning.

LAURA

SHE KNEW THAT she could go online for the weight loss support group, but the in-person meetings were so much better. The other sympathetic strangers who nodded when she shared her weight struggles were surprisingly reassuring. No one told her to just stay longer at the gym, like Dan had been for years. Not that she was looking forward to the weigh-in. She was shocked at the first meeting when everyone actually got on a scale in front of the whole group and said the number out loud. She had been too afraid to get on a scale for years but her size had slowly but surely gone from a four when she first met Dan in college, to a current size twelve. Not hugely overweight like some of her support group, but she was only five-foot-two and each of her four pregnancies had left her with a total of twenty-five pounds that she didn't want.

Her eating plan did not go well over the weekend. In the process of examining her food triggers, she now realized that the scene with Dan had left her vulnerable.

She walked in the house on Friday afternoon, expecting to find the boys with a snack in front of the TV. Instead, she heard the sound of soft jazz playing over the music system. The dining room table had a white linen tablecloth on it—she didn't even realize they had a cloth for it—and was set with wine glasses and a vase full of pink and white gerbera daisies, her favorite flower. She could smell garlic and onions being sautéed in the kitchen. The scent aroused her hunger before she saw what was going on—Dan was there. Her stomach clinched in a knot.

He walked into the entry where Laura was holding a grocery sack.

He walked toward her, reaching for the bag. "Let me get that." Out of habit she let him.

"Where are the boys?" was all she could think to ask.

"Sam is next door with Rhonda. Jessie took John to a movie after school, and then they are going to Rhonda's too. Don't be mad, please. I just wanted a chance to talk to you alone. To tell you how sorry I am and how much I miss you."

It really was infuriating how little Dan had aged over the years. He still had a thick head of wavy brown hair, hardly any grey in it, and was as trim as ever. He was wearing her purple striped apron and his unsure smile left him appearing nervous. She liked to see him that way.

"Okay, you told me." She didn't want to make this easy for him.

"Can I cook you dinner?" he asked.

"It smells like you already are."

He smiled again, this time fuller, showing teeth. She hated the fact that she still found him attractive.

"I'm sorry if I bombarded you, I didn't know how else to get your attention." Dan walked back to the kitchen and Laura followed him. "You don't have to stay in the kitchen with me, but please let me cook for you."

She had cooked dinner most nights for the family for the last twenty-five years. She packed lunches for the boys, prepared homemade dinners that could be eaten in the car on the way to the almost constant soccer practices. Just when she thought it would let up as the older boys could fix more of their own food, Sam came along. It all felt never-ending and with Dan out of the house it was only amplified. Last week she had resorted to eating off paper plates.

"What are you making?" she asked, letting her gut speak for her as it growled.

"Chicken cacciatore. Remember, I used to make it for you before the boys?"

She did, in fact, remember. She remembered the very

first time they ate chicken cacciatore together. He had brought it to his office for her in a Tupperware container, still warm, with two plastic forks. They had met there late in the evening and had made out in his easy chair before feeding each other.

"Yes, you did. Leave it in the kitchen. I'm not eating with you tonight."

She walked out of the kitchen and went up the stairs to their bedroom. As she stripped off her sweaty gym clothes and threw them in the laundry basket, she allowed herself to remember the rest of that night in Dan's office with the chicken cacciatore.

They had finished eating and were fooling around and taking sips of the scotch Dan kept there. Drinking scotch made Mimi feel so much older and sophisticated than her nineteen years. She was unbuttoning his khakis when his office phone rang. Her memory played it in slow motion—she reached over to answer, he shook his head wildly—No!—and stretched across the desk to try to stop her.

"Dr. Thomas's office. He is *busy* right now, if you know what I mean."

Her giggles at first concealed the sound from the other end of the line. After she stopped giggling she realized what she was hearing on the other end was a woman sobbing. She hung up the phone, horrified. That's how she found out that Dan was married.

CASSIE

SHE HAD OVERSPENT at Target but really wanted to make the apartment look homier. A new bedspread, a colorful lamp, a throw blanket to snuggle on the couch with, and a proper set of dishes. She was unaccustomed to eating at home, after so many years of eating for free at the restaurant. When she had started cooking in her tiny one-bedroom apartment, she realized she had very little in the kitchen except for water bottles and cereal bowls. Creating her cooking space, complete with Japanese knives and a Vitamix blender, was satisfying. One year of law school under her belt and she was finally feeling like a grown-up.

She got out the vacuum cleaner The other activity competing for her time was starting her reading in constitutional law. She had energy to burn even after her run and wasn't ready to get settled in for the night of boring reading. The second year of law school was supposed to be the hardest, she'd been told for years, but she wasn't worried. She and Jacob could help each other study.

Someone pounded on her door and she stared at it,

startled. She almost never had any visitors. Thru the peek hole she saw her Aunt Maggie texting furiously on her phone. Cassie pulled open the door reluctantly.

Maggie looked up and smiled. "Well, hello sunshine!" She burst through the doorway past Cassie.

"Hey, Mags. What's going on?" Cassie looked nervously around the living room as Maggie passed through.

"Not much. I've got the night off so I thought I would finally check out your new digs." Maggie walked around the sparsely furnished apartment and into the kitchen. She opened cabinets and peeked into the fridge. "Very nice. I'm impressed. This place is a million times better than the crash pad I called home in Queens for five years."

"Thanks. I like it. I'm still trying to get it right, but I think it will be just fine. I love not having to park on the street." Cassie kicked a pair of Jacob's running shoes under the couch while Maggie had her back turned. She glanced at his duffel bag under the small round dining table.

Maggie dropped into one of the two chairs by the table.

"Want a beer?" Cassie asked. It was the only beverage she had to offer other than coffee. She opened the fridge and took out two bottles of IPA.

"Sure, thanks." Maggie took one of the bottles. "So, how long has Jacob lived here anyway?"

Against her will, Cassie felt her cheeks redden. She didn't know why she felt apprehensive to talk about it. "About a month." She sat down with Maggie and took a long drink from her beer. She had to limit herself to just one, she thought, too much reading to get done tonight.

"Does your mom know?"

"No. It's not that I'm hiding it really, but she never comes here. You know how she's been—I just don't know how she'll react. I'm being stupid. I'm an adult. It's just weird." She sighed and took another long drink off her beer. It could end up being a short night of reading if she kept this pace.

"Not stupid, my dear. You are the opposite of stupid. This has been a tough time for everyone, especially your mom. Give her some time. She'll come out of it."

Cassie looked skeptical. "Yeah. I guess I didn't think it would take so long." She finished off her beer.

"Grieving is wrestling with a terrible beast. But you know that." Maggie put her hand on Cassie's shoulder.

"But I have Jacob and I have school. Mom just keeps showing up to work, doing what she has always done. Just without Daddy." Cassie rose from her chair, letting Maggie's hand fall off of her shoulder. "I don't know how she can go there every day. I mean, I find it painful to be there. I'm reminded of him everywhere. I can't wait to leave but it's the only place I can spend time with her." She opened the fridge and pulled out two more bottles. She set one in front of Maggie and opened the other for herself. One more wouldn't hurt.

"This too shall pass. Your grandma used to say that to us all the time."

"Anyway, I'm really happy with Jacob," Cassie said, smiling and pulling her wavy hair behind her ears. "It's actually nice talking about it with someone. But enough about me. How about *your* love life? Anyone special?" Since Cassie was a little girl, she had loved to listen to Maggie talk. Her mom tended to be quiet and withdrawn; her aunt was the opposite.

"Well, I'll tell you that it was a lot easier meeting men when I was flying. It's hard to get out there when I'm in the kitchen all the time." Maggie opened the second beer for herself and checked her phone for new texts.

Cassie leaned over the table, getting close to Maggie's face to get her attention away from her phone. "There are plenty of men in that kitchen, even some cute ones. I know how this works, Mags. Who have you hooked up with?"

"Discretion please! I do not kiss and tell." But she had a sly smile on her face as she put her phone back in her pocket.

"Come on, you can tell a little bit. We're family. . ." Cassie knew there had to be some juicy details.

"I will tell you that Bobby isn't into girls, but you probably already know that. And Evan is unremarkably endowed downstairs." Maggie held up her pinky finger and shook her head.

They laughed. It felt good.

"Pedro, on the other hand, is a great kisser. I may get into trouble with that one." She fanned herself.

"He's the prep guy, right? With the dimples?"

Maggie nodded and finished her beer.

"Isn't he a bit young?" Cassie asked. "He looks about my age." She thought he actually seemed like he could be younger than she was, but didn't say it.

"Well, it's hard to tell with the Mexicans and I haven't exactly carded him, although there have been what could be considered a frisk or two. . ." They laughed. "But I don't think I'll get arrested."

"We should double date some night when you are off." Cassie clasped her hands together with excitement.

"Simmer down there. We haven't gotten to the date stage." Maggie went to the fridge and grabbed another beer.

Jacob came through the door, carrying a bouquet of flowers in one hand and an enormous book in the other. He saw them and smiled, the faint lines around his green eyes crinkling. He was growing his blond hair out, the way Cassie liked it, so that he could be mistaken for a surfer dude who somehow ended up in Oklahoma.

"Well, lookie here, two of my favorite ladies in one room." Jacob walked over to kiss Cassie and gave Maggie a hug. He handed Cassie the flowers and winked at Maggie. "It's our year anniversary tomorrow."

"Jeez, Jacob, such the romantic," Maggie teased.

Maggie grabbed another beer for Jacob.

"Let's see what you have going on here," he said, gesturing to her new ink on her biceps.

Cassie sat back and listened to them chat. She had been first attracted to Jacob strictly based on the package he was born in. They had kissed at one of the first law school parties she went to last year, but it had gone so much deeper. After her dad died, she was so lonely and confused. Without his constant presence, she didn't know how she would have stayed in school She couldn't imagine her days without sharing them with him. Now it was her turn to be there for him. With his parent's current crisis, he was so worried about his little brothers and his mom. But he was laughing and gesturing wildly as he talked to Maggie, and Cassie felt contentment wash over her.

She was feeling so peaceful, in fact, that she let the words come out of her mouth. "Maggie, can you keep a secret?"

JOYCE

SHE HAD THAT awareness that she was dreaming, how you can understand that what was happening wasn't real—she knew that—yet she relished the time warp that was slumber. It was where she spent time with Andy; she didn't want to wake up. Often she relived a scene from their daily life together: trips to the grocery store to pick up needed items for the restaurant, laughing while eating Cheetos from the bag while walking down the aisles, hiding from customers; massaging his back and shoulders as he stood in front of a simmering pot; huddled around their computer, strategizing on a trip to Australia. She saw herself there with him in dreamland, could experience her happiness in the moment, taste the artificial twang of the Cheetos, feel his muscles surrender to the pressure of her hands, smell the garlic that could never be scrubbed completely from his hands. Yet she knew that she would wake up and be alone.

The worst part was not opening her eyes. She had grown accustomed to the emptiness of her bed. Not smelling coffee when she brushed her teeth, that was the worst part. Andy had brought coffee to her first thing, having almost always awakened first. He would warm up her mug before filling so that it would stay hot. His smiling face in front of her—he was such a morning person—a kiss on her neck, the smell of coffee on his breath. Andy. Her marrow ached for him as she brushed her teeth.

At the restaurant yesterday, as Joyce was picking up a credit card from a table that needed to leave quickly, someone from the next table had asked her a question. This was a customer who had moved away, an older lady who went to Florida to be closer to her grandchildren. Joyce couldn't remember her name but recognized her face. She grabbed Joyce's arm as she was walking by to stop her. Joyce hated to be grabbed at by customers, even sweet old ladies. It was even worse than being snapped for. She was feeling hurried to run the credit card for the other table, which might explain why she failed to go to her default answer.

"Hey, Joyce, where is that handsome husband of yours? I'd love to say hi before I have to go. If it's not too busy, will you ask him to come out?"

She froze and couldn't remember what to say. The only thing she could think of was, *He can't come out, he's dead.* She knew that wasn't the right thing, and in those awkward moments of silence she asked herself, *What do I say? I can't remember, what do I say?*

She finally muttered, "I'm sorry," and walked away. Someone else would have to tell her. She found the server, handed her the credit card from the other table, and retreated to her office.

She had her appointment with her therapist Amy in an hour. At least she would have something to talk about with her now. She only went to appease Maggie, who told her months ago during her snap that if she didn't get therapy, she would stick in her the loony bin for thirty days. That was enough to get Joyce speaking again.

She had passed over twenty days in her house, not uttering a single word out loud. It wasn't that she didn't want to talk, it felt like she physically couldn't. But Maggie's threat had punctured her silence. So now she went to therapy every week and spent the morning prior trying to invent some measure of progress she could share with Amy.

Amy was thrilled with the news of the marathon training with Cassie. "Good for you, I'm proud of you for agreeing to do it." Amy wanted to talk about her future. "Close your eyes and imagine the restaurant one year from now. What do you see?" Amy wanted to talk about the past. "Can you tell about that day?"

She could not talk about that day, didn't know if she ever could. And while the appointments with Amy seemed to her to be a waste of time and money, she did realize that Amy did offer her one suggestion that she followed. "If you can't talk about it, maybe you could draw it?"

She had been an art major in college before her early marriage ended. When she left him and left school, she also left her art behind. Until last month, she had not held a sketch pad in over twenty years. As she held it, her hands trembled with her pencil while trying to draw the closet door. She got as far as the reflection of the lamp on the shiny brass doorknob.

She kept the sketch pad locked in the safe with the bank deposits.

JACOB

GETTING BACK TO Oklahoma City every week proved to be more challenging than he had first thought, back when he promised his mom over a month ago. The drive was more than an hour from Tulsa, each way, and the gas was getting expensive. It had helped financially when he moved in with Cassie, but he hated having to accept her money. She had gotten a payout from her father's life insurance policy and didn't think twice about sharing her credit card with him.

The best drives were when Cassie would come with him. They would talk or listen to the radio or just stare ahead toward the road while she ran her fingers through his hair at the back of his neck.

He tried to time his visits so that he could catch one of his brothers' games. Jessie was playing varsity football as a wide receiver, John was on the JV team at running back, and Sam was in the soccer little league.

Cassie would wear one his ball caps—to look sporty, she said—and cheer loudly, whether she knew what was going on or not. She didn't know much about team sports, hardly knew the rules, really. She had run track in high school and her parents were not sports enthusiasts, one of the consequences of working nights and weekends, she told him. But having her at his side relieved the stress of having both of his parents in the crowd.

His dad would come over to greet him as he was standing by his mom, then turn to say, "Hello, Laura. You are looking well." She wouldn't even look at him.

This was the most extended silent treatment he had ever witnessed, and he had seen a few over the years. His mom didn't tell him what happened this time, but it must have been a doozy. The only one talking was Sam, who at six years old had not yet developed the family filter.

"Daddy's coming home soon," he told Jacob while in the drive-through line at Dairy Queen during his last visit.

"Really? How do you know?" Jacob asked.

"He told me he wants to. And I can hear Mommy crying in her room when she thinks I'm asleep. I think she misses him."

But Jacob wasn't so sure. The only thing she talked about with him was her weight loss plan and exercise goals. She was envious of Cassie's marathon training with her mom. "Wouldn't that be fun for the two of us to do it together?" she asked him. He couldn't imagine his mom running a 5K, much less a marathon, but he smiled and said yes. Her determination to improve herself made him wonder if she would ever take his dad back.

His dad mostly asked about his studies and about Cassie.

"You know, your mom used to look just like that," he told him, nodding toward Cassie in her ball cap, screaming with enthusiasm. "Tiny. Beautiful."

"She's still beautiful," Jacob said about his mom in her defense. And she was, really. He had at least three friends over the years who had admitted they had a crush on her.

"Yes, of course she is. And even more than that, she's an amazing woman, an incredible mother." His father pursed his lips and for the first time ever, Jacob thought he looked gaunt. He wondered if he had been eating.

"What happened this time anyway?"

"Oh Jacob, I know you're a man now, but these things are complicated. It's not easy being married, you know?"

He didn't know; the thought of being married to Cassie was exhilarating.

"I've been taking your mother for granted. I've not been careful with her feelings. Things came to a head." He shook his head in what appeared to be real remorse.

You've been fucking your students, he wanted to say. But what stopped him from saying it was not fear of his father's reaction. Pity is what stopped him. He had always looked up to his dad and his intellect, but now couldn't help thinking that his father was the most stupid man he had ever known.

MAGGIE

"THIS IS NICE, getting out with you in someone else's restaurant for a change." Maggie looked across the booth and a bowl of chips and salsa at Joyce.

Joyce was looking better, stronger; most certainly her new running schedule was having a positive effect. That was a brilliant stroke of Cassie's asking her to run the marathon with her. Fresh air, sunshine, being around other runners—and in San Diego no less. She had no doubt that Joyce would be able to run it—if Joyce could do anything, she could complete a goal.

As a kid Joyce would knock on every door in a twelve-block radius selling Girl Scout cookies; eight years straight she sold the most boxes, so proud of the special badges she earned it was almost ridiculous. Her ability to focus had always been daunting to Maggie.

"Do you have anything spicier than this?" Maggie asked the waitress, pointing to the small crock of salsa.

"It is nice, Maggie. Thanks for inviting me." Joyce took a sip on the salted rim of her margarita. "But this tastes like a powdered mix," she said with a frown.

"Yes, agreed. Not bad, just not good either."

The waitress brought a green salsa to the table, which to their delight was much spicier.

"So, there's a reason I picked this place to come to," Maggie started with.

"Uh oh, that sounds ominous. Does your boyfriend work here?" Joyce asked, looking over her shoulder. Maggie glared at her. "No, *you* work with your boyfriend. Don't worry, I know all about dimples. Nice catch."

"This has nothing to do with dimples, well not directly anyway." Maggie leaned over closer on the table. "Although, he is pretty cute, isn't he? Mercy."

"Wow, I think I almost saw you blush. Just keep it out of the kitchen. Sexual harassment works both ways you know."

"Ya, ya, whatever. I think you've been to one-too-many human resources seminars. Besides, I know what you and Andy were up to when you were doing inventory in the storeroom alone. And look—I think I almost saw *you* blush."

They looked at each and laughed.

"So, *anyway,*" Maggie continued, "this place is regarded as the best place in town for Mexican. Kind of a dump, don't you think?"

"Yes, I was surprised you wanted to meet here actually. I haven't been here in years."

"We don't have to stay to eat, but if you recall, everything is covered with an inch of melted cheese in here. I don't think they even order any fresh vegetables. It's the kind of food served in a college dorm. This is considered good Mexican."

"Yes, it's lame. And . . ."

"Stay with me here. You and Andy created a beautiful space and, for the time, a great menu. But that was years ago. The demographics have changed, I'm sure you have heard that the brown people will soon outnumber the whites in America" She paused, feeling nervous now that she had launched in.

"Yes, I listen to NPR too."

"So, I wanted to float an idea past you. Just something to think about."

"Okay. I'm all ears. What is it?"

"Let's update Andy's Café. Let's turn it into a modern Mexican taqueria. I've been to these cool places on both coasts where the food is so simple, but delicious and pure. I think it could really go over well in Tulsa."

Joyce looked down at her hands and for a while said nothing. Maggie waited; she was worried that Joyce might start crying.

Finally, she looked up. "Let me get this straight. You want to destroy the business that Andy and I built with our own two hands? The one that has provided a job for you on and off for years? You want to give it an *update*, maybe give your boyfriend a better way to express himself? Is that what I'm hearing?"

"Stop it. You know Andy wasn't afraid of change. Come on, this is about a business opportunity."

"This is about your inability to stay the course. This is about you, once again, getting bored and wanting to shake things up. And you want to tell me how my husband felt about business now? This is unbelievable."

The waitress stepped up to the table, looking oblivious to the obvious tension. Maggie pointed at their half empty margaritas, non-verbally ordering another round.

"So, do you want to order food now?" the waitress asked, irritated.

"Terrible service," Maggie muttered, shaking her head.

Joyce drained her margarita. "Do you want to give your notice? I can find someone else to run the kitchen. Is that what this is really about?"

"Jesus, no!" Maggie tried to calm down, to control her urge to lash out in anger or sarcasm. "This is about trying something new. This is about acknowledging what a good run you've had and moving on. This is about beginnings. Don't you think you could use a new one?"

Joyce let tears fall to her cheeks. It was the first time Maggie had seen her cry since their mom died. She had remained dry-eyed even through Andy's funeral.

"Fuck you, Maggie," she said, with the tears still flowing. "You have no idea."

At least now she felt she was getting somewhere. "Okay, then tell me. Of course I don't know what it's like to come home and find your husband dead of a heart attack, or whatever the hell happened. You are going to have to *tell* me. Please, give me an idea of what's it like."

"It wasn't," Joyce said, and then she stopped herself.

Maggie waited, shoving a chip with a mound of salsa on it into her mouth. *Don't interrupt her. Maybe she will actually open up.*

But her mask dropped back into place, and without even wiping the tears from her cheeks she lifted the edges of her lips in an attempt at a smile. "I'm sorry, Maggie. I overreacted. I'll think about it, I promise."

Maggie's heart sank, not because she thought Joyce wouldn't go for the new food concept, but because she thought the window to her pain had budged open a bit, only to be slammed shut again.

"No worries, you know I love you. But since we're here, I guess we could get drunk and eat a pile of cheese?"

Joyce laughed, her tears still clinging to her jawbone. "Yes, let's drink and eat cheese."

"I can text Pedro and see if he could drive us home later. It's too easy to get a DUI these days. Since you hold the liquor license, you need to be careful."

"You text each other, do you? Oh my, this is more serious than I thought," Joyce teased, scanning the menu.

"Well, of course, I text him. How else is a girl able to make a booty call? Or is it called a booty text now?"

And they laughed and they drank and later a friend dropped Pedro off at the restaurant so he could drive the sisters home. And after Maggie invited Pedro in and she was thinking back on the night with Joyce, all she could think about was what a shame it was that Joyce couldn't finish her sentence to explain what she meant by "it wasn't".

LAURA

FRANKLY, LAURA WAS surprised that Dan agreed to go to marriage therapy. He never would in the past, and when she had asked him this time, it was more of a taunt than a real desire. Showing up would only force her to acknowledge what she had suspected for years but was unwilling to deal with. Nevertheless, they had an appointment scheduled for next week.

As she packed the boys' school lunches, she glanced at the phone to see that she had missed a call from Jacob. He probably was calling to tell her he couldn't come up for the game tonight. Now that his classes had started, his time was getting so precious. She knew she should release him from the sense of obligation he had to visit weekly, to be the man in the house for his brothers. But she couldn't bring herself to do it, not yet.

She loved when he came, if only to have some adult conversation. Jessie and John were in the distant teenage phase of not talking much to her, and when they did, it was usually just asking where they had left something. Or if the laundry had been done. "Mom, have you seen my shoulder pads?" "Mom, where is that sheet with my training schedule?" "Mom, is my jersey clean?" And Sam had such a sweet nature, but he was only six years old. She could see the worry on his face when he talked to her, so she tried to keep his schedule and routine just as it had always been.

But Jacob was different. Mothers didn't have favorites of course, they would never admit to such a thing, but Jacob had been such an easy child. Eager to please, but relaxed and fun—she was so proud of him. And he looked like her, with his light coloring and blond hair, not like his father, which especially now, was a relief.

The truth was, she really missed Dan. She didn't know if she could hold out much longer keeping him out of the house. For all of his faults, he was a good listener, would even nod and act interested when she told him about her day. Her only friend was Rhonda, but she didn't want to dump everything on her, she had her own problems. Laura had few people to talk to and she looked forward to seeing Jacob when he made the drive over to be with the family. She missed the way Dan read out loud to Sam before bed, even when he chose some pretentious bullshit like Shakespeare to read. His voice was assuring and soothing and she found it hard to sleep without hearing it. Poor Sam must be suffering without his readings too.

She also feared the direction things were going with her trainer. Thomas spent one hour with her twice a week at her gym. He was a shameless flirt—harmless, she had always thought. He would smile, flex, and wink for both men and women, whoever he was training would be the object of his attention. He was good at his job; he made tough demands but was encouraging. She had lost six pounds—his motivation was paying off!

But last week when he placed his hand on her lower back to keep it from arching during her bicep curls it lingered a bit too long. Then when he brought her a post-workout protein shake, his eyes lingered at her ample cleavage, so obvious it was almost laughable. And yesterday he got directly behind her as she supported the heavy squat bar on her shoulders. She could feel his entire body pressed up against hers. The part that worried her most was that she didn't move. She liked the way it felt to have his muscles up against her. She liked feeling desirable. She was unsure what she was capable of and didn't want to find out.

But instead of deciding how to handle her time with Thomas, she picked up the phone and called Jacob. It went straight to voice mail—he was probably in class. She left a message, "Hey there, honey, I saw you called. Hope to see you tonight. I know John would be disappointed if you weren't there. You should see his new buzz cut, he looks like he's in the Marines or something! Anyway, call back if you need to. Love you."

She had planned on giving him an out to coming to the game—"Don't worry about it if you are too busy studying" or something. But a guilt trip came out of her mouth instead. She almost called him back but was interrupted by a text dropping in.

Dan wrote, "Appointment is confirmed for Monday at 3:00. See you tonight at the game. Miss you."

She didn't respond. She went to get the journal she kept by her bed. It was full of an assortment of information: vacations she had taken, books she had read or wanted to read, weird dreams, funny things her kids said. She turned to a new page and wrote "Marriage Therapy" at the top. She wanted to try to think straight when they were there and not let Dan control the conversation. He was so cerebral that he could easily maneuver a professional.

Whenever she wanted clarity, she made a list. First on her list she wrote "Amber" and under that she wrote "How many others?" Then she wrote "Sex/Intimacy."

She stopped to chew on her pen. Ever since that night when Dan surprised her with the chicken cacciatore, she had been thinking about the beginning of their relationship. After much thought she finally wrote, "Dan's pattern. What about Joy?"

JACOB

JACOB WAS INDEED calling his mom because he didn't think he could drive over for his brother's game. But it wasn't because he needed to study. Cassie wanted him to go on an early training run with her and her mother. She wanted him to be there when she told her of their plans. It had been the first real fight they had.

"Why does it have to be Saturday morning?" he asked. "You know how late these games get over, and then I have to hang out with everyone for a while. Do you want me driving home by myself in the middle of the night?"

"Can't you skip a week?" she asked. "Do you have to go *every* week?"

"Only if I want to keep my word. Come on, Cassie, my mom and brothers need me. Do you want me to say one thing and then do another, like my dad?"

"No, of course not. It's just so hard to schedule time with her. This is our first long run together and it would be nice if you were with us."

"How long is the run?"

"Twelve, I've mapped out that loop around the lake."
She grabbed her phone to pull up the route to show him.

"Twelve? You guys have been training for the
marathon, not me. I am in no shape to run twelve miles,
especially after going to OKC and back the night
before." With exasperation he dropped his hands to his
side. "Are you trying to kill me or something?"

Cassie stopped suddenly and looked up at Jacob. The
vein on her neck bulged and pulsed blue under her
translucent skin.

Jacob put his arms around her. "I'm sorry. That was a
stupid thing to say."

She relaxed her head down on his shoulder. "It's okay.
I'm too sensitive, I know. Daddy wasn't killed, he just
died. I just that I still don't understand."

Jacob didn't either. He had just started dating Cassie
when Joyce found Andy dead in the shower. A healthy
man who loved to box, was trim, and didn't smoke.
Dropping dead from an apparent heart attack at fifty-
one? He didn't have high blood pressure or cholesterol
or blood sugar or anything off. Cassie wanted her mom
to have an autopsy but Joyce wouldn't do it. Since
Andy had been adopted as a baby, he didn't know
anything about his birth parents; maybe there had been

a genetic condition.

"Let him have his peace," she told Cassie, which only infuriated her.

"What about my peace?" she had asked Jacob.

"Let me check in with my mom and see how she sounds." Cassie nodded into his armpit. "I love you, my sweet Cassandra. Everything is going to be okay." And he even believed it when he said it.

JACOB

LAST YEAR. . .

EVEN THOUGH HE thought the experience of being in a fraternity during his undergrad years was lame at best, his membership in the frat meant enough to him that he went back to visit for homecoming weekend. His buddy Seth practically begged him to indulge in a night of drinking beers with the younger guys in their house. He had just started his classes in law school, even met a girl he was interested in, certainly had no desire to relive those days, but ended up going anyway. Seth wore him down and he decided he could see his family while he was there.

After he and his brothers played putt-putt and went out for pizza, he met Seth at the frat house. Still smelled like piss and cologne.

"I'm out of here, man," Jacob said to Seth, after too many high fives, fist bumps, and luke-warm beers. "It was good to see you."

Seth's eyes grew wide, "No way! You can't bail on me now. Things are just starting to happen."

"I know, I know. I'm heading back tonight, though. I've got a ton of reading. I don't want to fall behind."

Seth put his arm around Jacob's shoulder. "Just one more at the Pike. For old times' sake."

The Pike was the hole in the wall bar on campus that had been serving beet to under-aged kids for decades. It was dark, hot, and smelled like puke.

"Okay, one at the Pike, for old times' sake," he agreed, thinking he could lose him quickly once he got there.

They walked the six blocks to the bar, the crisp autumn air giving energy to their beer-soaked limbs. As usual, the Pike was packed and sweltering.

"First round's on me," Seth said, grinning and elbowing his way to the bar.

Jacob let Seth push his way ahead while he found space on a wall to lean against. He felt old as he looked at the crowd of posturing co-eds who appeared as if they could be friends of his brothers. He pulled out his phone to check his messages and scrolled through, hoping that Cassie might have texted. He was waiting until Monday to reach out to her, trying to play it cool.

"Anything interesting?"

He looked up and saw the cute, smiling face of Amber. They had met last year, even went on one date before Jacob decided she was too much of the cheerleader type for him.

"No, not really," he answered, putting the phone in his pocket. "How are you doing, Amber?"

"Great actually! Semester is off to a good start. How's law school?"

"So far, so good." Now he really wanted to leave. Getting away from her could prove to be more difficult than ditching Seth.

"This is my friend, Ellie," Amber said, nodding at the brunette next to her.

He shook Ellie's hand and looked over her shoulder to find Seth. "Well, it's nice to see you, Amber and to meet you, Ellie, but I. . ."

"Jacob is Professor Thomas's son," Amber told Ellie. "Remember me telling you about Professor Thomas?" She had a devilish grin on her face.

Ellie suddenly seemed interested in the conversation. She looked at Jacob, checked him out from head to toe. "No kidding. He's cute too."

Jacob blushed. "Thanks, I guess. Anyway, see you guys around. I'm going to find my friend."

"Wait!" Amber said, handing her beer to Ellie.

Jacob paused and Amber grabbed his face in her hands and a planted a long, slobbery kiss on his lips.

He gaped at her surprised—they hadn't even kissed on their date the year before.

She let go of his face and smiled. "Thanks Jacob!" She turned to Ellie and giggled.

Bewildered, Jacob just stood there with his mouth open. Amber and Ellie turned away and huddled with their backs to him.

"So, does he kiss like his dad?" Ellie asked Amber.

Jacob closed his mouth and stared at their backs.

Amber laughed. "I know it was stupid, but I couldn't resist. Father and son!"

Jacob turned to leave, not even finding Seth to say goodbye first. He couldn't bear to hear another word.

DAN

DRINKING AN AGED single malt scotch had always been an indulgence for Dan, but recently it had become more of a requirement to get through the night at the hotel. He was trying, for the first time really, not to get himself entangled with another girl. That was how he thought of them—girls.

They were old enough to bear children but these young women all fell under that category. Even Laura was a girl to him once. It wasn't Laura catching him with Amber that caused this change in game plan. Well, it may have been part of it, but the other part was seeing his son Jacob with his girlfriend Cassie.

She was the age of many of his former girls. She was also pretty enough, smart enough, and had the air of confidence that he would have noticed if she had walked into his class. After months of hearing from Laura about this new girlfriend of Jacob's, he surprised himself when he finally met her in person. Instead of the itchiness of desire that would often boil to the surface when around a girl like that, he felt paternal toward her. He wanted to protect her.

She had recently lost her father. Of course that must have had some influence on his feelings toward her. But he had been with girls who had daddy problems before and it always ended with him only making their issues worse. She was special, he could see that, and he felt relieved Jacob had found someone like her. But it only highlighted the poor choices he had made, the special one he had taken advantage of all these years. Maybe marriage therapy would help. At this point he would do whatever it took.

He was afraid he might fail the next test that came his way. Last night he was stretched out on the plastic pool chair, watching his boys make cannon balls into the indoor hotel pool and nursing a scotch when the texts started dropping in.

"It's Amber. Are you still at the hotel?" *Shit, he had blocked her number. How did this get through?*

"Don't freak out. Using Hannah's phone. I'm lonely." *Me too.*

"No strings, can I come over?" *Shit. Don't respond.*

"I failed my Chem quiz. Could use your attention." *Oh, she's just a girl. Like Cassie.*

"I know you think about me." *Try not to.*

"Hey, Dad!" Sam yelled from the side of the pool. "Watch this!" He jumped and created a small splash.

"That was lame," Jesse yelled. "Try again!"

"Last chance," the screen told him.

"Bye" was the final word, with a frowny face at the end.

He turned back to watch John push Jesse in the deep end, then proceed to try to dunk Sam in the shallow end.

"No dunking. Never hold someone's head under water. You know the rules," he said, walking to the edge of the pool.

He left the phone on the table next to his scotch. Why bother with it anyway? Laura didn't return his texts and Amber knew how to push his buttons. He was smiling at his boys, enjoying their unrestrained, rambunctious energy when someone came up behind him and pushed him in the deep end with a bump of his palm. Dan came up for air and grinned at John, who was laughing from outside the pool. He was fully clothed and completely drenched but didn't care. This was the most hilarious moment he had in ages, to be caught off guard and in the middle of fun. He pushed the water off of his face and threw his head back and laughed. He wanted to press the pause button on life and savor this moment.

"That was a good one. You really got me that time."

CASSIE

IT WAS THE perfect day for the long run—early but nothing obscene, clear sky, sunny but not hot, dry as a bone. Their feet stepped on the first of the falling leaves, crunching as they passed.

"Mom, your pace is great. I'm really impressed." Cassie checked the mileage on her watch. They just passed the three-mile mark. She had always assumed she had gotten her athletic gifts from her dad; now she was thinking that it might have also been from her mother's latent abilities.

"I'm sure I'm holding you back. Go ahead if you want." Joyce's deliberate, careful strides kept coming. "I can always turn on my music." She gestured to her phone strapped on her bicep. "I know you said they discourage having earplugs in during the race, but it helps me a lot for training. And I've never even run twelve miles before today. If I finish, that is."

But Cassie knew her mom would finish—or drop trying. It often became a head game completing these runs, not giving up mentally. And her mom was nothing if not stubborn and persistent.

"I'm glad we could do this one together then. I wanted Jacob to come too, but he went back home last night. A lot of family stuff going on there."

Joyce didn't ask for details and Cassie didn't offer any. They ran in silence for a while.

"There's something I wanted to talk about with you." Cassie's heart was beating much faster than was warranted by the run.

"Okay, sure. I may not respond much though, talking requires using my limited energy."

"You know how much I love Jacob. He's great, isn't he?" She didn't wait for Joyce to respond. "And Daddy didn't know him very well, but they had met, and I know he liked him."

Joyce nodded in agreement.

"And since his death, I can see that every day is precious. There are no guarantees for tomorrow."

"Very true."

"And you know I've always loved the idea of a destination wedding."

Joyce quickened her pace.

Cassie just trotted along with her—she was hardly breaking a sweat even with all the talking.

"So, what I'm trying to tell you is that Jacob and I are engaged. We want to get married in San Diego before the marathon. Isn't it all so exciting?"

Joyce stopped running and looked Cassie in the eye. "You dragged me out to mile six to tell me that you are getting married?"

Cassie glanced down at her watch. "Actually, we're just starting the fourth mile."

"You dragged me out to mile *four* to tell me that you are getting married?"

"Yes. I wanted you to be forced to talk about it, so that you can't walk away from me."

"Well, I think you have a bright future as a lawyer. You should file away this ambush technique."

"Mom, I just want you to be happy for us. Is that possible?"

Joyce took a deep breath and started running again. Cassie caught up to her easily.

"What's the one and only piece of advice I have given you about getting married?" Joyce asked.

"Hmm. Always have a credit card in your name?" She gave Joyce a hopeful look. Joyce didn't even crack a smile.

"Finish school first," Joyce said in shorter breaths. "Finish school first."

"Mom, I'm not destined to repeat your mistakes. I'm going to finish law school with or without Jacob. If I made it through last year, I'm going to finish."

Joyce stopped running and turned to Cassie. "You don't know what heartbreak can do to you until it happens. Being betrayed can leave you feeling like you're a different person altogether."

"Jacob isn't going to betray me, Mom. He loves me. He wants to spend the rest of his life with me."

"I know he does, and he is a great guy, I know that. But why rush the wedding? Get your degree first, then have the wedding."

"Remember, there is no guarantee for tomorrow, every day is precious? Don't let your own regret over not getting your degree punish me. I already *have* my undergraduate degree. This is where you introduce your cautionary tale, right? Your own failed first marriage?"

"I'm so sorry to bore you with details of my life. But you're right. I don't want some of them repeated in yours. Getting married while you are young and still in school isn't easy. You haven't grown up yet. You aren't fully formed."

"I'm sorry your first husband was an asshole, that he broke your heart. But Jacob isn't. And you did meet Daddy, right? It did end well, didn't it?"

Joyce put her hands on her thighs and leaned over, staring at the ground. Cassie recognized the slow breaths and loud exhales her mom took from the years of walking by her on a yoga mat in their family room as she tried to relax from a stressful day. She knew her mom could continue with her controlled breathing forever and didn't want to wait it out.

"Mom, it's really important for me to have your support." Cassie's chin was quivering, and she clenched her jaw.

Joyce stood up and started running again. "What mile are we on now?"

Cassie ran up next to her. "Still on four."

She was determined to stay at her mom's side until they finished twelve. Leaves were crushed under their shoes as they continued. Cassie waited for her mom to speak—she preferred to think in silence, she had told Cassie since she was a little girl. Her dad, on the other hand, had liked to talk to get to his thoughts. Their runs together had been full of conversation. Her mom stopped suddenly to remove her shoe and shake out a small pebble that had worked its way in. Without a word they began to run again. Cassie glanced at her watch—into mile five.

"I suppose San Diego in May is lovely. Were you thinking a beach ceremony or something?"

And that was enough for Cassie to feel like she had her mother's blessing. She went on to spend the next eight miles telling her how she saw the wedding. Nothing too formal, she might even wear flip-flops and certainly no tuxedos. Yes, a beach, even if it was raining she wanted to be near the ocean. No flower girl, but maybe Jacob's little brother could be ring bearer with a beach ball or something. Wouldn't that be cute? And on and on she went, happy to bask in her mother's attention.

JOYCE

MORE THAN ANYTHING, her feet hurt. Thinking she could work full-time on them and run a marathon at her age was probably a fantasy, but at least it gave something other than work for her to focus on. For inspiration, she read articles on the internet of people in their eighties running their first marathon. Taking time for stretching and strength training was recommended for older runners. It became unreasonably important to her to finish the race. She knew it was out-of-balance somehow for her to care so much, but it didn't bother her if she were displacing some unmet emotional needs by putting one foot in front of the other, for hours on end. Elusive metaphors were of no concern to her. She just would keep going, even if it hurt.

Those twelve miles were not only tough on her joints, however. Now her heart felt bruised too. All she wanted to do was talk about it with Andy, who would have lovingly talked her back from the ledge of her fears. She could almost hear what he would tell her, holding her hands, smiling. . . *It'll be okay, lighten up, Cassie is a smart cookie.* Joyce replayed these imaginary words in her head, as if they were real and could reassure her, still craving an actual conversation, an actual touch. But she wasn't much for those graveyard scenes, talking to the ground as if it were a person, like they did in the movies. Andy was cremated anyway, his ashes hidden in the storeroom of the restaurant because she didn't know what to do with them.

"Just drop my ashes off the edge of some dramatic cliff," he had said years earlier, when dying didn't seem like a possibility for any of them. "And for God's sake, don't bury me. Those funeral directors should be arrested, the way they exploit the grieving. And then there are the environmental issues with burial . . ." And on he went, his hands waving as he talked, his freckles making him look so much younger.

So, it was an easy decision for Joyce to choose cremation. But she hadn't yet found that dramatic cliff and deep down didn't know if she was willing yet to surrender those ashes back to the earth.

She removed her sketchbook from the safe, locked the door to her office, and sat down with it at her desk. She opened it to the page she had been working on and was disappointed to see she hadn't completed more—there were only the outlines of a door and a shiny doorknob. She turned the page to start over. Forget the door, she thought, I'll start with what I saw when I walked in the bedroom.

She began with the bed, king-sized with a simple blue blanket. There were four pillows in white pillowcases propped up against the wood headboard. None of those fussy throw pillows, purely for decoration, but the bed was made and neat. Except for the enormous pile of clothes dumped at the foot of the bed. Clothes on hangers, seemingly removed from the closet. She finished drawing the pillows and was starting her first hanger. Someone was trying to open her office door. Then came an insistent knocking.

"Why is the door locked?" Cassie asked from the other side. "Are you in there, Mom?"

Joyce quickly shut her sketchbook and put it back in the safe. She opened the door, smiling at her daughter. "Sorry, I was preparing a deposit in here. There is a lot of cash from the weekend and I didn't want any of the staff walking in on me." She wished she hadn't lied to her daughter but didn't want to tell her about the drawing.

"Oh, I see. At first I thought maybe Maggie had locked herself in here with Pedro." She laughed.

Joyce could tell she was in a good mood, relaxed.

"Better get that in the bank soon. But at least the safe is bolted down now. Remember when, what was his name? Dale? When he picked up the safe and shook it to dump the contents out? Just got a few checks. I hope he ended up getting some treatment."

"Yes, I remember Dale very well. I wanted to press charges but your dad said just to fire him, that the natural consequences of his life would be punishment enough. I don't know what happened to him."

Cassie was holding her book bag and laptop—she was either coming or going from class.

"What's going on?" Joyce asked. Cassie rarely stopped by without a reason.

"I wanted to ask you something. Jacob and I were talking about how we would like to have our parents meet. I was wondering if we could do a dinner here? Just his parents and brothers, us, and Maggie? Before you say no, that it would feel like work to have it here, I want to tell you why I want to." She paused. Joyce noticed that her freckles had become more prominent over the summer. "This has been my second home really, and it somehow feels like Daddy would be here."

How could Joyce say no to that? "Sure, of course."

"And I want to show off Jacob to everyone here." She laughed again, and then hugged Joyce. "Thanks, this means so much to me. I'll talk to Theresa about reserving the back room. Is Saturday okay with you?"

"*This* Saturday?"

"Yes, this Saturday. It works for their family, and they have a million games and things they have to schedule around."

"Sure, if the room is available, this Saturday is fine. I'll be there with bells on." She did a little jig, enjoying the happiness of Cassie.

"I'm going to go talk to Maggie about the menu. I was thinking the *osso buco* would work, that the boys wouldn't find it too weird."

"Make sure you set the time early if you want Maggie to be able to sit down at all. Saturdays usually get pretty busy after seven."

"Yes, thanks for the reminder. I'll see if we can do five. Oh, I'm so excited!" She suddenly stopped, her face serious. "I forgot to tell you, Jacob's parents have been separated for the past month or so. I think this will be the first time they will sit together for a meal since their separation. We're hoping it might help things between them, get them in the same room around family and all. And that our love will be contagious." She was beaming.

When Cassie said things like that, Joyce remembered how young she really was—thinking that their engagement could save another marriage. But, who knows, maybe she was right. Maybe love was contagious.

"Thanks for the warning. I'll do my best to inspire contagious love. Oh, and I know you love the tiramisu but it was taken off with the last menu update. Too tired, Maggie said. But we can make it for Saturday if you want, just be sure to mention it to her."

"I will, thanks again, Mom. This means so much to me," and she bounced out the room.

Joyce was left with her aching feet and her locked safe. She did not return to the sketch she had started before Cassie interrupted her; instead she got online to order a new pair of the thick-soled running shoes.

MAGGIE

MAGGIE WAS IRRITATED that Joyce told Cassie to order the tiramisu for her group on Saturday. A group she was expected to join nonetheless, and on a Saturday, the busiest day of the week. The reason she took tiramisu off the menu is that she didn't *want* to make it. Let them have the mascarpone tart with hazelnut brittle that was on the menu. It was so much better anyway.

But at least the engagement cat was out of the bag and Maggie didn't have to tip toe around her conversation with Joyce that involved Cassie anymore. There were plenty of other areas of conversation to avoid with her as it was. Any change at the restaurant for one. They had not talked any more about the modern Mexican concept that she had brought up. She was waiting for Joyce to do it, but feared she might never.

Then there was the whole subject of Andy. Maggie thought that Joyce might like to reminisce about him, telling funny stories from when they all worked together. One afternoon after the lunch rush, Maggie launched into a memory of Andy with his hands held up like a surgeon having just scrubbed, covered in cocoa powder up to his elbows from the tiramisu recipe, asking, "Who's next for the proctology exam?" Maggie mimicked how Joyce had leaned over and raised her hand and they laughed. But other times a cloud would fall over her face and she would walk out of the room. Maggie was fatigued from the constant walking on eggshells around her. *And then*, she goes and has Cassie order the shitty tiramisu, which she swore off ever making again once it came off the menu.

But she could ask Pedro to make it. She was his boss, she could ask him to make whatever she wanted, and he was actually a really good cook. But she knew that he would do it without her even asking if he knew she didn't want to. He wanted to please her. It was so refreshing.

She sought him out in the basement prep kitchen. He was cutting onions, methodically and quickly, into a small dice, and then scraping them into a six-quart container. She watched his back. Small statured with broad shoulders, he was tight and strong. Even in his baggy black cooking pants, she could envision his frame. Worried she might indeed be robbing the cradle, she finally asked him how old was. Thirteen years younger, not a problem for either of them. It was always Joyce who was drawn to the older guy.

Although they were alone now, she decided not to grab his ass as she walked by. Who knows who could walk in, and besides she would want to finish what she started. Too much work to do.

"Joyce is driving me crazy," she said as she leaned her back against the stainless table that he was working on.

He shook his head slightly. "Sisters." Coming to America from Mexico as a young child, he only had a slight accent. God, it was sexy.

"I wish she would let me do my own thing. She is such a control freak."

Pedro just nodded and kept on with the onions. She knew he wouldn't join in on the trash talking of her sister. He liked Joyce, telling Maggie early in their relationship, "She has kind eyes."

"I mean it was always Andy who had the vision around here."

"I'm sure she just misses life without him," he offered, never pausing from his onions. He had such a poetic way of speaking Another sexy thing about him.

"Well, *I* miss him too. He taught me how to work the line. Before I was flying, I worked here on and off. He was with me when I got that rainbow tattoo on my shoulder when I was eighteen. He agreed with me when I told Joyce that she should drop her awful nickname 'Joy.' He was my brother, you know." She didn't realize until she started talking about Andy just how much she missed him.

Pedro put down his knife. "Yes, he was your brother. I'm so sorry he was taken from you." He took her hand. They stood there holding hands until they heard footsteps coming down the stairs. She squeezed his before she dropped it. As she walked away she went ahead and grabbed his ass for good measure.

What Pedro said was just how it felt to her—like Andy was taken, snatched up in the prime of his life and no one could figure out what to do with the gaping hole that was left.

LAURA

SAM STAYED HOME sick from school on Monday, giving Laura an excuse to reschedule their therapy appointment. His coughing had kept them both awake, leaving her tired and irritable. She texted Dan, the first communication she had initiated since he left.

"Sam's sick. Can we reschedule our appointment?"

He responded quickly. "Yes. I'd like to see him. To give you a break."

"I'm fine. I'll just order pizza for dinner. Can you pick up Jesse from practice at five-thirty?" She hated to ask him for anything, but it was too far for Jesse to walk.

"Yes, of course." Then a minute later, "Next Monday, same time. I'll take care of dinner tonight." And because she had eaten two Pop Tarts that morning and didn't want to eat pizza that night, much less get on her scale for her scheduled weigh-in, she decided to let Dan make dinner for them.

Laura spent the day spreading vapor rub on little Sam's chest, getting him drinks of water, pressing a cool cloth on his forehead. Then when he slept, she did the laundry, went through the huge stack of mail she had been ignoring since Dan was gone, and sorted through the many sheets of paper the boys brought home from school. There were notes to sign allowing them to ride the bus for field trips, letters from the nurse needing updated immunizations, a request for ten dollars for the band sheet music. She felt like burning them in the fireplace and going to bed. She even had to cancel her training appointment at the gym.

So, when Dan showed up with Jesse at around six, with a bag of groceries and an eagerness to please, she was actually happy to see him. She didn't feel cut out to be a single parent, didn't think it would be so hard with the older boys in high school. But having her day disrupted by Sam being sick had rattled her. Once Dan walked in the door, she welcomed Jesse home and promptly went upstairs to take a nap. She knew it was late in the day for such an indulgence, but didn't care. She might be up again with Sam and his coughing.

She woke up close to eight and garlic was the first smell to hit her senses, quickly followed by bacon. She wanted to cry they smelled so good. Spaghetti carbonara, it had to be, it was one of her favorite dishes. Back when she ate carbs, that is. Not on the approved eating plan, not a *diet*, of course, they didn't call it that anymore. No, more like a Wellness Lifestyle Overhaul or some other bullshit. Having started the day with junk food, she decided to allow herself the pleasure of the pasta. She brushed her teeth and hair and went downstairs.

Dan was on the couch, reading out loud from a book. She couldn't see the title, but it didn't sound like Shakespeare. He was sitting in the middle, John on his left, Jesse at the far, right end, and Sam nestled in his lap. She hadn't seen the older boys listen to Dan's story time in years. They appeared to be hanging on his every word. Dan used varying inflections with the different characters, really throwing himself into the portrayal. For several minutes they didn't even notice her standing there listening.

Eventually, Dan looked up and saw her in the doorway. He smiled broadly. "Is it okay to go to the end of the chapter? It's really getting good."

"Sure, of course." She walked to them and sat in the easy chair that was next to the couch.

Not listening to the words, she watched the expressions on their faces. Sam's eyes were droopy and glassy-eyed; she guessed he might fall asleep any minute. Jesse's eyes were growing large, as if he couldn't believe what was about to happen in the story. John wore a smirk, like he had guessed what was going to happen and was proud of himself for being so clever. And Dan wore contentment like a top hat.

He closed the book and carried Sam up to bed. Jesse

and John went upstairs to shower and get organized for the next day. Laura rose to go find some food and as she turned the corner to pass through the dining room, she saw the table was set for two, with wine glasses, candles, and the same tablecloth that was used on chicken cacciatore night.

"Can I try again?" Dan asked from the doorway. His contentment still shone.

Laura thought that she should say no, to tell him to go to hell, but she found that she didn't want to. She wanted to sit down at the table with him and eat some delicious unsanctioned food, rattle on about the trials of her day, and listen to the sound of his voice. Thinking she was weak, but surrendering anyway, she simply said yes.

And their dinner was so comfortable, so delicious, and so reassuring to her that even though she had no intention of doing so, she surrendered in other ways too.

As Dan was clearing the table, Laura began to fill the dishwasher, both of her hands holding a stack of plates. Dan came up behind her and placed his hands on her waist. Not sensing any resistance, he pulled himself behind her close. Laura could feel that he was hard. He reached under her shirt from behind, and first unclasped her bra, then took her breasts in his open palms. She felt like she was on fire, even the touches from her trainer

Thomas couldn't compare. He tickled her nipples with one hand and reached between her legs with the other. He seemed in no particular hurry; it took all her restraint not to open his zipper. She let him go for as long as he was willing to, in so much pleasure that it was difficult for her to continue standing. When his hands finally reached for her shoulders to turn her around, she stopped them.

"No, stay there. Stay behind me for it." So he did, in front of the kitchen sink, pants around his ankles. It was the best they had had in years.

But hearing noise on the stairs, they scurried to get clothed. John walked in to get a drink of orange juice.

"Well, I guess I should go," Dan said, a hint of a question at the end of his sentence.

"I guess so," Laura said.

She wanted them to sleep in their bed together, have a night of spooning, even have Dan get up with Sam if he needed a drink of water. But she didn't want to confuse the boys; she needed more time to think about all of this.

Letting Dan come home had been on her mind all day. Seeing her family together felt so good. But she didn't want to rush to any decisions. And she certainly didn't want to have one hot sexual encounter sway her.

Because when she thought of hot sexual encounters, her mind flashed to the scene between Dan and Amber. Amber had probably made plans based on Dan's performance too. And while Laura may have once been a young college girl impressed by the displays of attention from a teacher, those days were long behind her now.

LAURA

THE FEW HOURS that Sam was in kindergarten, which unfortunately was only half-day, instead of the full-day like many schools, were precious to Laura. It was the only time that she had to herself. She guarded this time possessively, trying not to schedule any appointments or other commitments. She was unaccountable for these hours. Dan went off to work, the boys went off to school, and until she picked up Sam at noon, Laura did as she pleased.

Early in the week she would focus on housework: keeping the laundry going, scrubbing the toilets, grocery shopping. By Wednesday or Thursday, if things were looking good at home, she would allow herself a little treat. Shopping for a new pair of sunglasses, a pedicure, a latte in her favorite bookstore.

Today she took a kick boxing class at her gym that was exhausting, so she rewarded herself with a stop at the new frozen yogurt shop that Dan had taken the boys to but she had yet to try. "You should see all the toppings!" they had told her. She made a deal with herself as she pulled into the parking lot—only have the fresh fruit and avoid the candy bars. Reaching into the back seat to get her purse out of her gym bag, she noticed what looked like Dan's car on the far side of the parking lot. Squinting, she could see his parking permit on the back windshield and recognized his license plate. Why would he be here at eleven a.m.? The boys were all in school . . .

She went for her phone and almost dialed his number before she stopped herself. His car wasn't even close to the yogurt shop; if he were in there he could have parked where she had. She looked at the other shops in the strip mall: a dry cleaner, an accountant's office, a veterinarian, an Indian restaurant, a jewelry store. Aha—maybe he was shopping for her birthday! It was only a few weeks away, and Dan was always good about gifts. But he wasn't really parked close to that shop either. He must be there, why else would he be parked in this area?

She decided to give him a few minutes to get back to the car before she surprised him. She went inside the yogurt shop—the kids were right, there were so many toppings. Giddy with the thought of a new piece of nice jewelry, Dan always had excellent taste, she went ahead and got some candy bar toppings on the chocolate-mint frozen yogurt. Her first bite was delicious in her mouth, cold and creamy chocolate with the nutty, crunchy chunks.

She took a couple of bites but stopped herself from finishing it off as she walked across the parking lot. She wanted to save some for Dan when he got back to his car. She was rehearsing what she would say when he came back to the car with a bag from the jewelry store. "What are you doing here?" while giving him a chance to hide the bag. Or, "Did you have a hankering for fro-yo too?" Or maybe she should just let him leave and not ruin the surprise? No way, she thought, it would be too much fun.

She walked across the parking lot, treat in hand, enjoying the warmth of the sun on her skin. She had gotten a chill from the combination of still wearing her sweaty clothes and eating a frozen dessert. She decided to wait inside of Dan's car to warm up and wondered if he had bothered to lock it. Typically, he didn't lock his doors, he always told her he just didn't leave anything valuable inside.

Her hand was reaching for the handle of the passenger side door when she noticed movement inside the car. It was the first time she even bothered to look into the window. And there was Dan sitting in the driver's seat, hands gripped on the wheel, head leaned back, eyes closed, mouth open. She thought he might be napping until she saw where the movement was coming from. A blond head was bobbing up and down on his lap.

JACOB

CASSIE SAT AT their kitchen table, chewing on her pencil as she read the application to intern at the Legal Aid clinic. Jacob grabbed a container of hummus, ripped open a bag of pita chips and joined her, returning to his reading on trusts and estates. It was staggeringly boring. Cassie kept bringing up the family dinner, and while he was grateful for the distraction from his reading, he was beginning to wonder if this dinner was a good idea. She had been so excited—he loved to see her so happy—so he had been going along with it. But it was Wednesday and he felt he needed to tell her.

"I haven't told them about the engagement yet." He had intended to the previous week, but tensions back home were running high. He was worried it wouldn't be received as good news. He hadn't told Cassie one way or another, but she had assumed they knew.

"Why not?" Her face fell.

"Because everyone there seems miserable, that's why."

"Don't you think the news might improve their mood?"

"I'm not sure either of my parents are enthusiastic on the subject of marriage right now."

"Do you want to cancel?" She had been so excited about this dinner; he was touched she would even offer.

"No," he said, reaching for her hands. "Let's do this. I think we should just save the good engagement news for that night."

She stood from her seat, walked over, and sat in his lap. "Perfect, thank you." She nuzzled her face in his neck. God, he loved that.

"Besides, my brothers are totally hyped about coming for it. I promised that they could drink all the soda they wanted. You should have heard them asking questions. 'Is Cassie able to eat there for free?' 'Can you order anything you want when you go there?' They are very impressed my girlfriend's family owns a restaurant."

"You mean your fiancée's family. Isn't it weird saying that out loud?"

"I know, right?"

They giggled and practiced saying fiancée.

Jacob extended his arm forward. "Here is the soon to be Mrs. Jacob Thomas," he said in a British accent.

Cassie's smile froze in place.

"What? So, maybe I need to practice the accent."

"It's not that. It's just the name part. I always thought I would keep my name. I guess we haven't ever talked about it." Cassie got up from his lap and returned to her chair.

Jacob had never even thought about it, actually. He assumed she would take his name. His mom had taken his dad's after all. "Oh," was all he could come up with.

"I mean, you know I'm an only child. So was my dad. What will become of the Beckers? What will become of my dad's name? Even he's gone now."

"I know, you're right. I'm not sexist or anything; it just feels weird. I don't know what to say. It wasn't what I was expecting."

Cassie's eyebrows furrowed. "There are four of you Thomases. Four. All men with no fear of *your* name dropping off the face of the earth. Why don't you take Becker if you are so enlightened?"

He could see her point, certainly. But there was no way he was going to take Becker as his name. The guys he knew would think he was a complete pussy.

"Or how about we both hyphenate? That seems the most fair," she offered.

"I went to school with a couple of kids whose parents

did that. Don't you think it's obnoxious to ask your kids to use Thomas-Becker their whole lives? Or is it Becker-Thomas?"

"No, I don't think it's obnoxious. No more obnoxious than expecting me to drop my lineage."

They sat in silence for a moment. Who cared about a name when he would get to be with Cassie for the rest of his life?

Jacob bowed and said in his awful British accent, "Here is the soon-to-be Mrs. Cassandra Becker-Thomas."

Not a bad ring to it, actually.

DAN

HE WAS AS good as in now. After what happened at the kitchen sink, he felt certain it was only a matter of time. He couldn't remember feeling so elated. Initially disappointed he didn't spend the night at the house, as he had been planning ever since Laura said he could do dinner, he quickly felt like it was better to leave. Give her something to stew about, maybe she would actually *ask* him to return.

Not that he was staging the whole night there. When his older boys wanted to listen to him read, that's when he realized how much he needed to fight for his marriage. Not simply getting laid—that had been too easy and available to him for years now. Yes, he wanted to have Laura, almost as much as when he first met her, but now he wanted her to want him. And he wanted his family back, to be in his own home, to wake up in his bed next to Laura. He was still surprised he had been so careless with it all.

So, he got his hair trimmed—Laura liked it short. He let his facial hair grow—Laura thought it looked sexy. He went to the gym five days in a row—he wanted to look strong. He even trimmed his toenails because it grossed her out when he neglected them. He wanted to be in tip-top shape for the dinner on Saturday.

This dinner was going to be when they reunited; he just knew it. When Jacob first asked him to come, telling him how important it was to Cassie for their families to meet, he was initially skeptical. The thought of pretending everything was fine for some strangers made him tired. But these were strangers who Jacob wanted to impress, who Jacob loved. The hostility he had been feeling from Jacob since the separation had been especially painful. He had always thought Jacob was most like himself and that they shared an easy camaraderie. His cold shoulder hurt. He would do whatever Jacob wanted him to. That was why he first agreed to go.

And then he realized that acting out the family scene, even if forced, was exactly what would draw Laura back. He saw the look in her eyes when she was watching him read to the boys. His physical presence in their house was a turn on to her. Yes, he would come to the dinner and he would be irresistible. That's why he was feeling so damn good. He was convinced that he was as good as in.

DAN

DAN HAD NEVER left campus with one of his students before, but Amber had been relentless. "Not in your office *again*," she complained, and pouted with her beautiful mouth. She hinted that she would make it worth his time if he would just take her for a drive—"I lost my virginity in a car, you know. . ."

Why he had stopped in the parking lot with the frozen yogurt place, he couldn't say—no particular reason, he was just anxious to get things going with her so that he could get back on campus, where he felt comfortable. Amber was beginning to wear him out, stopping by his office unannounced, sending him pictures of her tits; she even called him late at night when he was at home last week. Clearly, they had just about run their course together, but he couldn't resist one last illicit meeting before he broke things off. And everything was going so well, she had started in on him while he was still driving, her hand down his pants almost immediately. He was feeling so good there parked in the lot with Amber working him over that even after he saw his wife's face through the passenger's side window, his first inclination was to smile and wave.

He had never seen that expression on Laura's face before. Horror. Pain. Fury. She ran off and drove away before he had the wherewithal to even get his pants up. He jumped out of the car and promptly stepped in a dish of frozen yogurt spilled on the ground. Cursing, scraping a chunk of candy bar from his shoe, Amber emerged from the car with a furrowed brow.

"Hey, what's going on?" she asked. "Did I do something wrong?"

"You didn't see her?" he asked, incredulous.

"Who?" she asked, truly clueless.

"My *wife*. She looked in the window and saw us."

"Oh. I didn't see her." She shrugged and smoothed her hair down. "Should we at least finish what we started?" She nodded back to the car.

"Are you fucking crazy?"

She put her hands on her hips. "What's your problem? Haven't you always been married? So now she knows."

"So now she knows? That's your response? She is my wife, the mother of my children, I actually love her."

Amber used a fingernail to pick something out between

her teeth. "You have a funny way of showing it, Professor."

Dan grabbed her by the shoulders. "This. . . what we've been doing. . . all of it, Amber. . . it's over."

She pushed his hands away "God, you are such a pussy. And a lousy kisser; Jacob's better." She put her hands back on her hips and put her mouth back into its pout. The fact that he was turned on by her pout just heightened his anger. How *dare* she say that about his son? In a reflex—the thought hadn't even entered his mind to strike her—but before he knew what happened he had slapped her hard across her flushed face. He had never hit a woman before, never so much as pushed one in anger. And for the second time in five minutes, he was thoroughly disgusted with himself.

CASSIE

SHE AND HER mom were on their long run for the week, this time for fifteen miles. It was early Thursday morning, the sun just peeking over the horizon when they met at a city park. Cassie was really impressed with her mom's training. The piece of paper she printed off as a training schedule when she gave Joyce the shoes was laminated and on a clipboard in her office. She clearly intended on finishing this marathon.

Cassie had no agenda for conversation for this run, really just wanting to get it behind her so she could focus on all of her reading. Then she needed to prepare for Saturday's dinner. They often ran together with extended periods of silence and weren't bothered by it. Sometimes her mom even listened to a book, her earbuds firmly in place. But today Cassie wanted to talk.

"How many can fit at the large round tables?" She really wanted to get everyone at one table for the dinner. And round tables were so much more intimate.

"We have a couple of the table toppers. I think you can get up to ten at those."

"Well, let's see. There are five of them, the two of us and you and Maggie. Excellent, that should work then. I'd like to push the other tables back in the storeroom if possible."

"I don't know, honey. Since we are eating so early, we might seat tables in there later in the night. We'll make it private for our dinner and then open it up. Maybe we could set the tables and push them against the far wall? Then we can have a quick turn around."

"Okay, that's fine. I don't want to lose any more business than is necessary, especially since this ticket will be comped. But I did ask Jacob to talk to his dad about tipping the server at least. I'll make sure it's enough."

"That was thoughtful of you. But I can take care of it if they don't." Both of them were very sensitive to having the staff wait on them, wanting to make sure their employees were abundantly compensated.

They ran in silence for a couple of miles. Cassie liked the pace, very easy-going. As the morning was unfolding before them, they saw the ordinary beginnings of their neighbors' day. A woman in her robe going to the curb for the paper, an old man walking his poodle, a man starting the sprinkler on his lawn.

A thought entered Cassie's consciousness out of the

blue, and it overflowed into a question to her mom. "Where are daddy's ashes?"

"What made you think of that?" Joyce asked, startled.

"I don't know. Maybe thinking about Jacob's family. Maybe it's this dinner. I'm not sure."

Joyce didn't answer right away. "I have them, of course. They are safe."

"That's good. But I wasn't worried about something happening to them, I just wanted to know where they are." Her voice started to rise. "I'm just realizing that I have never actually seen or held them. You didn't want them to be a part of the service."

Joyce maintained her steady running pace. "Dad isn't in there, you know. It's just a box."

"I know. Where are they?"

"It's an unremarkable, small, heavy box. Trust me, it's not a spiritual experience to hold the box."

Cassie stopped by the side of the road. "Why won't you tell me where his ashes are?"

"I just don't understand what the big deal is about them. I've got the box. I've been trying to figure out what to do with it."

"That's fine. I just want to know where it is. Where he

is?" Cassie wanted to yell, but held it in.

"I told you, he's not part of those ashes. You won't find him there."

"Where are the fucking ashes, Mom?" she shouted.

"The box is at work," Joyce finally answered. "Since he spent most of his life there, I thought having his ashes there for now seemed fitting."

"I want them," Cassie told her, not even sure why she said it. She turned to start running again; she had too much to do that day to stop any longer.

Joyce caught up to her. "I understand that you are upset about this. It's a completely normal reaction."

"I'm sensing a 'but' coming up."

"I'm not giving you the ashes. Not yet."

"Why? I thought there was nothing spiritual about having them? Isn't that what you said?"

"I'm not ready. I don't know what else to say about it."

Cassie suddenly felt compassion for her. She had been so strong, was even running a marathon at her age because Cassie had asked her to. Maybe it was selfish of her to ask more of her. She had Jacob; her mom didn't have anyone.

"Okay, but tell me this. Where are they in the restaurant?"

"Don't worry, they're safe. When we decide what to do with them, they will be there."

Cassie didn't press her about it. She assumed that they were locked in her mother's desk or something. She probably would have been surprised to know they were shoved in the back corner of the storage room, on a shelf under a pile of old yellow napkins they no longer used because they changed the color scheme in the dining room.

"I'd like to help decide where we can scatter them. And I want to be there to do it too."

"Yes, of course. I want you to."

Cassie checked her watch. "We just finished mile six. How are you feeling?"

"I'll live," her mom said with a tight smile.

"You're doing great. Nine more to go. You got this."

MAGGIE

PEDRO DID END up making the tiramisu that Cassie wanted for the dinner. Maggie searched the walk-in refrigerator to see what he put it in. She pushed past boxes of romaine, quarts of heavy cream (noticing the expiration date was tomorrow), a twenty-pound bag of yellow onions, a sheet pan of par-cooked risotto that wasn't properly labeled (would have to write up Jim about that) before finally finding it. A hotel pan—way more than was needed for the nine guests at dinner.

"Will you have Joyce add tiramisu as a dessert special for tonight?" she asked Maurice, the shift manager. No sense in letting the staff eat the rest when they could sell it. "Tell her to put a count on it. Twelve."

Because Joyce had to update the computer with the tiramisu special, she ended up running late to the engagement dinner.

Maggie put on a clean chef's jacket and walked back to the private room without her. She supposed it looked fancy ten years ago, now it looked dated: shiny brass light scones on the wall, floral patterned wallpaper, chairs that needed repainting to cover the nicks. French doors allowed the room to be secluded from the main dining room, giving privacy. Usually the room was used for various business groups. On the weekends when it was busier, they also used it for overflow seating for the general public. Walking in, she saw Cassie at the round table, messing with an ice bucket. She had on a simple red dress, flattering but not tight. Her golden locks were loose around her face. Wearing more makeup than usual, she looked elegant and beautiful. Jacob was standing next to her, helping her plunge a bottle of champagne into some uncooperative ice.

"Oh, hi, Maggie," Cassie said, "We were just trying to get a chill on this bottle. For the toast."

"Add some water to the bucket, that will chill it faster. An old flight attendant trick," Maggie suggested.

"I just got a text. They're on their way in now." Jacob looked around and grabbed a pitcher of water and poured it in the bucket. "Thanks for being here Mags," he added. "It really means so much to us."

"Are you kidding? I wouldn't miss this for the world," she said. Even though she was worried she would get called away if they got busy. She had told Pedro to come get her if things started coming off the rails on the line.

She knew they were coming before she saw them.

Close to the doorway she heard, "Shut up, Sam, don't be an idiot. You're going to embarrass Jacob."

"No, I'm not!" a young child's voice whined. "I just wanted to see the dishwasher. What's so dumb about that?"

An adult male's voice, surely the father's, said, "Boys, please. We are guests here. This is really important to your brother. Can we please hold it together for an hour?"

"That was a question, boys," a woman's voice said.

The mutterings of "yes, Dad" followed.

Cassie and Jacob rushed to the door to welcome them, giving hugs to everyone. Maggie lingered with the champagne, turning it in the ice to help it cool. She wished Joyce were in the room. She didn't like the pressure of being the sole representative of Cassie's family. She didn't want to go and hug these people she had never met but needed to regard as family now. So, she did what she had years of practice doing—she went into flight attendant mode.

She pulled the bottle from its bucket, gently untwisted the wire closure, and carefully covered the cork with a towel. It wasn't uncommon for corks to fly out without any coaxing; the towel would keep it close if that happened. She had learned the hard way, having almost taken out the eye of a passenger in first class years ago.

The group was huddled at the doorway, chatting, the teenage boys high-fiving with their brother. The little boy had already wandered off.

Maggie poured four glasses into flutes and carried them over. Smiling, she held them out to the group. "Welcome. I'm Maggie, Cassie's aunt. Shall we toast to the engagement?"

She reached over to hand the glasses first to Cassie and Jacob with her left hand, then to his parents with her right hand. She finally looked up, after having been very careful not to spill, and gazed up at the face of a slightly plump, but very pretty blond woman. This woman was standing with her mouth open, holding the champagne.

Maggie's first thought was that this woman had never seen a woman like herself with so many tattoos. With her tailored peach cardigan, she looked like a suburban soccer mom. Maybe she didn't get out much. She almost made a joke about it when the woman turned to Jacob and asked, "Engagement?"

Everyone stared at Cassie and Jacob, except for the little boy. He was running in circles around the table. Maggie couldn't believe it—no one had told her that his family didn't know about the engagement. Fuck.

Jacob quickly took charge. "Yes, engagement. I asked the love of my life if she would marry me and she said yes." He grabbed Cassie's hand. "That's why I wanted you to come tonight."

Jacob's mother drank the contents of her glass in one gulp. Maggie couldn't help but think that this meal might be more interesting than she had imagined.

"Congratulations," the man said, raising his glass, with his back to her.

Maggie realized she didn't have anything to toast with, so she turned to fill one for herself. One glass wouldn't impair her for working in the kitchen later. As she turned back to the group, raising her glass, Jacob's dad turned around too. Their eyes locked. Maggie saw the color drain from his face. She thought she might throw up.

"I'm sorry, I haven't introduced everyone to you, Mags," Jacob started in. "These are my little brothers, Jesse and John. Sam is running around the table. Sam! Stop running. You're going to break something. This is my mom, Laura. And this is my dad, Dan. Everyone, this is Maggie, she's Joyce's sister. Joyce is Cassie's mom. She should be here any minute."

Maggie tried to think of the last time she had seen Dan. From behind the wheel of her old Accord, waiting to pick up Joyce when she decided to leave for good.

Joyce came out the door with just one suitcase, leaving everything else behind, and climbed into her car. Dan watched her from the open front door. He didn't even try to get her to stay, or say goodbye, for that matter. Maggie had flipped him off as they drove away. He had barely changed in appearance in all these years. Although she didn't think she had ever seen him look so perplexed. He had been such a cocky bastard.

"Dan," was all that would come out. He couldn't seem to form any words at all. Movement in the doorway distracted her attention. Joyce walked toward them and paused to apply some lip balm.

All Maggie wanted to do was to get to Joyce first. She had to be warned, she couldn't just walk into this. But Jacob got to her first, put his arm around Joyce's shoulder, and brought her to the group. "There she is. This is my soon-to-be mother-in-law Joyce."

It was too late to do anything to stop it.

LAURA

LAURA WASN'T MAD that Jacob hadn't told her about the engagement, more disappointed. She had been so self-absorbed with her own problems lately, she hardly even asked about his life when she saw him. But she hated being the last to know. And having Cassie's aunt accidently break the news to them made her sad. Nothing some champagne wouldn't take the edge off though, it was a good bottle. And since she let Dan make the hour-and-a-half drive with them, she could over indulge if she wanted to. He could drive back.

The drive from Oklahoma City had been really nice. The boys were quiet, huddled over the respective electronics, headphones in place. The classic rock station was on the radio, songs they knew the words to, occasionally singing together. She was surprised how everything could fall back into place so easily, so comfortably. Looking at her children, how happy Jacob looked holding Cassie's hand, she couldn't think of a good reason not to go to therapy with Dan and get their family back together.

That's when she noticed Dan was looking ill. He looked

so pale it was alarming. The last time he had that coloring was when he experienced food poisoning a few years ago. He ended up in the hospital that time. But they hadn't eaten for hours and his champagne flute still looked full. She followed his eyes to where he was looking. A skinny middle-aged brunette was walking in the door. Cassie's mother, presumably. Her daughter apparently took after her father with her light coloring and the freckles. She knew that her dad had died recently, quite unexpectedly Jacob had said, so she wouldn't be meeting him. But she hoped to see a picture eventually. She wanted to imagine what her grandkids might end up looking like.

"Dan, are you okay?" she whispered in his ear. He wouldn't stop staring at Cassie's mom.

"It's Joy," he muttered to her. "Oh my God."

Laura could hardly hear him; she leaned over closer. "What?"

They were interrupted as Jacob brought Cassie's mom over to them, introducing her as his future mother-in-law, which sounded so weird to Laura's ears. How could Jacob have another mother besides her? It seemed like he was in kindergarten yesterday.

But Laura smiled and held out her hand. "Hi, I'm Jacob's mom, Laura. It's sure nice to meet you and thank you for having us all here tonight. Your daughter

Cassie is darling, you must be so proud." She waited for Dan to contribute to the conversation, but thinking he was ill, she continued to talk. "We just love it when she drives up with Jacob for his brothers' games. Don't we, honey?" She turned back to Dan, who was just staring like an idiot. Was he afraid he was going to faint or something?

The hand that Cassie's mom extended was limp. Laura took it and noticed it was trembling.

"Joyce," she whispered, not looking at Laura but at Dan.

Laura didn't understand why it seemed so awkward, *she* already knew about the engagement, didn't she?

Then Laura remembered what Dan just muttered when he saw this woman. Joy. She looked closely again at her. What some might describe as a handsome woman, not pretty in a conventional way, but attractive. But there was a gauntness to her, too thin, yet strong somehow. She looked to be Dan's age, since Laura was seven years younger, she had a good eye for older.

Joy, he had said. This woman wasn't smiling like she would expect, showing off at her restaurant with her beautiful daughter. In fact, she looked like she might cry. *It's Joy*, he had said, *oh my God*. But Jacob had just called her Joyce.

The woman with the all the tattoos, the aunt, Laura couldn't remember her name, burst in the middle in the group and put her arm around Joyce's waist. "I'm sorry, I need to steal Joyce away for a few minutes. Work emergency."

Jacob looked startled.

"The story of my life. There is always an emergency at a restaurant," Cassie said. "Some new guy probably set something on fire in the kitchen."

Laura laughed and was about to ask her what it was like growing up in the restaurant business, but she couldn't get Dan's words out of her head. It's Joy, oh my God. Joyce. Joy. It's Joy, oh my God. Joyce.

She thought of picking up that phone in Dan's office all those years ago. The woman crying at the other end. When she had hung up, no longer in the mood to continue fooling around, she asked him, "Who was that?"

"We need to talk," Dan had said, taking her hands in his. "That was Joy. My wife."

Over the years Laura tried to never think about this woman Dan had once married. When she did, she only thought of her as a voice crying. She had never seen her. She had believed Dan when he said that it had been over for a long time, that was why he didn't wear a ring, that she no longer even slept with him. The question that she had buried so deep that she had forgotten about it until this moment was—then why was she crying?

JOYCE

"I CAN'T GO back out there," Joyce told Maggie as she sat at her desk. She wanted to hide under it. She thought she might hyperventilate.

"Try to control your breathing," Maggie said. "Inhale, now exhale slowly."

With all of Maggie's years dealing with scared people on planes, she was very reassuring in a crisis.

Maggie joined her in breathing slowly, both trying to bring some semblance of control to the situation.

"What just happened? I'm having a hard time figuring out what's real right now." Joyce hadn't felt so disoriented since she found Andy in the closet.

"Dan is Jacob's father. Laura is his mother. I think I got that right. This is unbelievable." Maggie ran her fingers through her hair and left them clasped behind her neck to try to steady her herself.

"That marshmallow is Laura?" She remembered what Laura looked like back then. She had practically stalked her for a week before she came to her senses. Big hair with bold highlights, always tossing her head, petite and perky. But mostly she remembered how young she seemed.

"Yes, that was her. Dan's Laura. I can't believe this."

Joyce always imagined that Laura would stay beautiful and glamorous forever. She had pictured her in her mind as looking like Michelle Pfeiffer or Gwyneth Paltrow. Now she reminded Joyce of an elementary school teacher.

"Laura is Jacob's mother?" she asked, feeling dizzy.

"Yes. Dan is his father."

Dan. She hadn't laid eyes on him since she pulled away from their tiny house in Maggie's car. And while she spent the next eight months wallowing in the misery of their split, after she met Andy she rarely thought about him. Dan was mostly used as an example to Cassie about jumping in too fast in relationships. Their marriage had become, as Cassie liked to call it, her cautionary tale.

But coming face to face with him after all these years was a different matter entirely. It was infuriating how good he still looked. It would have been bad enough to have him and his family come in the restaurant, not knowing it was hers. But to see both him and Laura *and* find out that Jacob was their son; this she didn't know what to do with.

"Dammit, where the hell is Andy?"

Maggie didn't answer. What could she say?

"Dan and Laura are Jacob's parents?" She felt like she was trying to learn a foreign language, translating the incomprehensible into something she could understand.

"Yes, Dan and Laura are Jacob's parents," Maggie said.

"How could I have missed this?"

"Joyce, we all missed it. It's been a hell of a year."

"Jacob doesn't look like Dan." Maybe this was all some sort of mistake.

"No. But he does look like Laura. I never saw her before, but as they stood next to each other back there, I could see it. That little one, though, he looks just like Dan."

"I can't go back in there."

"No, but I should. Cassie will be walking in here any minute to see what's going on if we stay much longer."

"Dan and Laura are Jacob's parents?" Joyce asked again, maybe if she repeated it, she could convince herself it was true.

"I'll tell them you had to leave. Someone needed to be bailed out of jail, something like that."

"What are we going to tell Cassie?"

"I don't know, but I've got to go back in there. Are you going to be okay in here?"

Joyce nodded, but she didn't really hear the question. She was finally agreeing with the statement that yes, Jacob's parents were Dan and Laura.

She was surprised to find herself alone in her office. And for the first time for over a year she didn't crave any more space. For the first time in over a year she was lonely.

She had never felt the absence of Andy quite so sharply. She even forgot about Dan and Laura in the next room. The air around her narrowed so she no longer remembered why she was upset, the dinner that she was missing in the other room forgotten. The tunnel threatened to overtake her, so acute that, not knowing what else to do, she unlocked her safe and removed her sketchpad. She locked the door to her office and continued to draw the scene she had started. It wouldn't bring Andy back to her, she knew that, but maybe it would allow her to move past that image that she wanted to forget. Maybe by remembering she could better forget.

JACOB

HE SHOULD HAVE trusted his gut that this dinner was a bad idea. First, Joyce was late. Second, Maggie beat him to the engagement announcement. Then, Sam was running around like a mad man inside the restaurant, making Jacob nervous he going to destroy something. And now, Maggie and Joyce left, and his parents were acting so weird.

The server walked in with the salads, so they went ahead and sat down. Cassie launched in on a description of what was in it, but he wasn't listening. He glared at Sam and pointed down to get him to stay in his seat. Jesse started picking ingredients out with his fingers and putting them on the tablecloth. John picked up the discarded food and popped it in his mouth. They were acting like savages; why weren't his parents controlling them? He would never have been allowed to act like this in public. Staring at their salads, his parents didn't even seem to be listening to Cassie, nor were they eating.

His attention was diverted when Maggie sat down. "Sorry. Joyce has to have an address for an emergency. We should start without her."

Cassie looked pissed. "Is she coming back?"

"I don't know, I hope so. But let's eat." Maggie dove into her salad like she hadn't eaten in days. She wouldn't look up. Jacob now counted three adults staring at the table. He looked at his future bride and shrugged. What the hell was going on?

"What emergency, Maggie?" Cassie finally asked to break the silence. Sam surrendered his chair and started wandering again.

"Don't you mean Joy?" Laura asked. "Does she go by Joyce now?"

Maggie just sat there with her mouth open. Jacob couldn't believe it. She *always* had something to say.

"My mom did used go by Joy, actually," Cassie said, eager to start a conversation. "I only hear it rarely though, by people who knew her in college. How did you know that?" Her smile was full, she was so eager to please his parents.

"Stop it, Laura," his dad practically growled, failing in an attempt not to he heard.

"I heard of her in college actually, never met her though. Didn't realize that she was your mom until just now."

"No kidding? What a small world." Cassie nodded at

the server to remove the salad plates.

"Laura, can I see you in the other room please?" His dad forced out the stiffest smile he had ever seen.

"No, you may not."

What had crawled up his mom's ass?

"I didn't know her, but Dan did." Heads turned toward Dan in anticipation of how he knew Joyce.

"Have I told you all about when I decided to quit as a flight attendant?" Maggie interrupted. She didn't wait for a response. "A completely normal-looking woman was breast feeding her kitten. Yes, I said kitten. On the plane. Boob hanging all out." She looked at the boys. "Sorry, breast hanging out with a kitten on the other end. That was it for me."

"They can do that?" Jesse asked.

"Sadly, yes. I wish we could un-see things. That would be on the top of my list."

Sam picked up his pace, galloping around the table now.

"Thanks for sharing, Mags. Now I have to forever live with that image in my head." Cassie laughed and then turned to Dan. "So, do tell. How did you and my mom know each other?"

Before he could answer a Mexican guy from the kitchen walked timidly into the room. "Excuse my interruption," he said, smiling. "May I speak with Margaret, please?"

"He likes to call me Margaret," Maggie explained to the table, almost blushing.

"We could use you on the line," he added.

Jacob had never seen Maggie hesitate to respond to a work request, but she sat there like she was trying to decide what to do.

"Well, then, I better step out to check. It looks like your *osso buco* is up." Maggie left. The server entered the room, carrying large fragrant bowls full of falling-off-the-bone tender meat.

"Sam. Sit your ass in this chair." Jacob was unbearably irritated. Something about this meal was all wrong. "Sorry," he told Cassie, reaching for her hand under the table. She had a smile pasted on her face, but he could see a vein popping out on her neck.

Sam, finally in his chair, picked up the food on his plate by the large bone protruding from it. The meat plopped off the bone, splattering the demi-glace all over his light blue polo shirt and the surrounding tablecloth.

Jacob didn't want to yell so he said nothing. His parents were astonishingly mute. He couldn't even read the expression on his mother's face.

"Way to go, idiot," John finally said.

"No worries, little man," Cassie said. "My dad used to say that eating with one's hands provided a much more intimate experience with food."

And then his dad, with the same expression he had as when he delivered his grandpa's eulogy, cleared his throat. "There's something I need to tell you."

DAN

IT DIDN'T FEEL like he had a choice, really. When Laura got that crazy look in her eye anything could happen. He needed to control the message. It was bad enough; he thought by telling them now, he could prevent it from being worse.

But he lost their attention as he talked around the issue. The choices of our youth, the unintended consequences, the issues that adults protect their children from. Sam started again with his circling the table.

"Sam, sit down now or no iPad on the way home," he said.

Sam sat and started eating his *osso buco* with his hands.

"What are you trying to say?" Jacob asked him, clearly annoyed.

"What I'm trying to say is that I was married before your mom. For a very short time."

Laura's lips were pursed. She finished the wine in front

of her and then picked up Dan's glass too.

His kids at least looked surprised at the news.

"Okay, thanks for sharing," Jacob said. "Great timing to bring that up at my engagement dinner."

"He's not done," Laura said, taking a drink from Dan's glass of wine.

"That's true. You see, there is something else. It's not easy to talk about. Especially given the circumstances." He had never had such difficulty forming sentences.

"Dan, I think I may know where you are coming from," Cassie interrupted. "My mom was married before my dad, too. But I don't believe in some legacy of broken homes or anything. She's always harping on me about not getting married while in school, but Jacob and I have really thought about this. We aren't rushing into anything."

Dan's palms were sweating so much he had to wipe them on his pants. "I appreciate that Cassie, really I do. It's just that. . . Well, it's not always a straight line. I mean, things can get so complicated. You just don't know what. . ."

"You just don't know what, Dad?" Jacob asked.

"I mean, there can be these intersections that don't make sense."

"What isn't making sense is you, Dan," Laura said. She drained her glass then turned to Jacob. "Your dad is trying to tell you about his first wife."

"Listen, guys, you've opened up about your past, I get it. Can we please move on? This isn't the time," Jacob told him, then gestured to his brothers to stop texting at the table.

"He's trying to tell you *who* his ex-wife is," Laura continued. "Go ahead, Dan. Tell them."

All heads turned to him and he blurted out before Laura could, "Joy. I was married to Joy. I mean Joyce. Cassie, I was married to your mom."

Trying to read the faces of Jacob and Cassie, Dan was too distracted to notice that Sam had started with the running again. In fact, no one noticed until he collided with the server holding a giant tray of plates with tiramisu on them. The crash of the landing was followed by crying. First, it was Sam, who knew he was in trouble for sure. Then it was Cassie, who got up from her chair and ran out of the room.

CASSIE

SHE COULDN'T STAY in the restaurant—that was the one thing she knew for sure. She didn't go look for her mom, didn't head for the kitchen to see Maggie, she walked straight out the front door without looking back. Getting in the car that she and Jacob had driven over in together, she realized he would be stuck there without a ride. He would have to figure it out.

The words that were playing like a gong in her head were not what Dan had said. They were what she had said to her mom when she told her about the engagement. *I'm sorry your first husband was an asshole, that he broke your heart. But Jacob isn't.*

She drove to their apartment and put on her running clothes. Sitting on the couch, after lacing up her shoes, she found she couldn't move. And certainly not run. She stretched out and stared at the ceiling, noticing a water spot she had never seen. *Jacob's not an asshole, he's not like your first husband. He's not like. He's not like. His father?*

She turned on the music on her phone, put in her headphones, and played it loud, loud enough to drown her thoughts. She chose a song she loved in high school, an angry chick-song she knew all the words to, trying to resurrect the feeling of being so young and without cares. As if she had anything to be angry about when she first memorized these words when she played it over and over again in tenth grade.

She played it again and again, pacing the room, singing loudly, closing her eyes to surrender to its rhythm. And when she finally felt like she had the energy, she did the one thing she could always count on to clear her head. The one thing that required nothing from anyone else.

She went for a run.

MAGGIE

BY THE TIME Maggie got back to the private dining room, everyone was gone except for the server scraping tiramisu off the carpet.

He looked up at Maggie and said, "They didn't tip."

"I'll take care of it. See me before you leave." The room was a disaster—bowls of *osso buco* half-eaten still on the table, obvious spills on the white tablecloth, even a chair fallen and turned on its side. She shouldn't have left, she berated herself. Why did she leave?

She went back to the kitchen. The rush was winding down; only the dessert station was slammed now. There were plenty of people still on the clock to get the orders out. On the dessert plates lined up on the rail to be picked up by the servers, she mostly saw the tiramisu. Of course. Customers would probably order an Oreo cookie if she put in on the menu. She nodded for Pedro to follow her and then walked down the hallway to the utility closet. He followed her in.

"How could it get any worse for them?" She collapsed

into his arms. He felt so strong and steady. She loved the way he smelled, a combination of sweat and lemon. "I haven't told them yet." Her plan had been to tell them she was pregnant at dinner. She had been so surprised that her equipment was still capable of conception. Even more surprised by how excited she was by the news. How excited Pedro was.

"The right time will come, Margaret. You'll know when it does."

"Just when I thought we might all be able to move forward. Jesus, Dan is Jacob's dad. How is it possible Cassie fell in love with him, out of all the boys in the world?"

"Such a mystery love is, isn't it?" Pedro smiled at her and rubbed her shoulders. "Where is Joyce?"

"I left her in her office. Let me go see." She pulled all the cash she had in her pocket and handed it to Pedro. "Could you give this to Josh? Tell him I'll get him the rest tomorrow. That room is a nightmare. This whole night has been."

The door to Joyce's office was locked when she went back to check. She knocked lightly at first. "Joyce, it's me, let me in. They're gone." No answer. She pounded louder. "Do you want me to make a scene? Open this door." She considered asking Pedro to help her get in.

The lock clicked and the door opened before her.

"Where's Cassie?" Joyce asked. "I've been calling her, she isn't picking up."

"I don't know. The hostess said she saw her go out the front door."

They sat down at Joyce's desk. "Listen, I had to jump on the line for a bit to help. When I came back, everyone was gone. I don't know what went down exactly."

"You *what*?"

"I had told Pedro to come get me only if they got in the weeds. They needed me."

"Maggie, *I* needed you. How could you let this happen? So, we don't even know what they told her?"

"Well, excuse me. Your life is pretty fucking complicated. I was trying to take care of your business, so I wasn't available to take care of your daughter. Hello? This is your life, you know." It felt like she was in grade school again and Joyce was pissed at her for not curling the back of her hair correctly. You aren't serving me well, little sister. Maggie was so sick of it.

"And, by the way, what's the worst they could have said in there anyway? The truth?" She stood and walked out of the office.

She wanted to leave it all. Joyce and her problems—she had problems too. Did Joyce even care about those? Inwardly she fumed, back in the kitchen, throwing pans with more force that was necessary into the dish pit. She fantasized about living on a Mexican beach with Pedro and their child. She was imagining what skin tone their baby would have when Joyce's words from their last fight rang in her ears. *It's about your inability to stay to the course.* Maybe I can't stay *your* course, she wanted to tell her. Maybe she had her own course to stay on.

MAGGIE

AT THE END of a trip she was always dead tired. This particular international flight from Barcelona was especially draining. One of the other flight attendants was sick and not pulling his weight, making it hard on everyone else. She wasn't left alone for a moment, someone always needing something or even just wanting to complain about another passenger's body odor—which admittedly was awful. During the final walk through of the cabin she reached her fingers into her pocket for the smooth pieces of sea glass she had plucked from the sand on the beach during her twelve-hour break. She rubbed them superstitiously, hoping the tranquility of gathering them would transfer to her current weary, frazzled state. Her throbbing feet and short emotional fuse usually sent her in search of a few drinks—tonight was no different.

After showering in her hotel room, she went downstairs to the bar and sat with some of her friends who were working the same flight. It was a quiet gathering of a small handful of people who mainly wanted to be left alone for a while before re-entering the regular world. They were drinking, complaining about the passengers, telling jokes. Maggie felt herself start to relax when she ordered her third beer. As she lifted it to her lips, she saw Ben walk in the room, freshly showered in a polo shirt and khaki pants. She smiled—she hadn't seen him in ages. They used to have a similar schedule but when he was promoted to captain she rarely saw him.

"Hey stranger," she said to him as he sat down next to her at the bar.

"Thank God." He smiled, his green irises shone under tired eyelids. "I've had the worst day. To see your face, Maggie, I think my luck is changing." He ordered a shot of tequila and a beer.

"Yeah, I've had a tough one too. Are they really all so much worse these days? Or is it just me?"

"I don't know." He threw his shot down then followed it with half of his beer. "But I left the airport today hating everyone."

"I know the feeling. I'm not sure how much longer I can do this. I always thought I would be one of the old ladies still flying, but maybe I've had enough."

"I think that after every trip. Then ask myself, what would I do instead? Become a salesman?"

"I wonder if I could handle a normal job anymore," she

mused.

"Want another one?" he nodded to her beer.

"Sure. Maybe some peanuts or something too. I'm getting buzzed."

"Good. Right where I want you." He smiled, placing his hand on her lower back. She leaned back into it.

He ordered another shot and beer, a bowl of spicy peanuts were brought out. They ate them, kept drinking, watched the TV at the bar showing a college football game, occasionally kissed. They had enjoyed a few nights together in the past; it felt comfortable to mess around.

Maggie realized after a while that everyone else was gone. It was hard to tell how much time had passed, coming off of a long flight. And plus, she felt drunk. The kisses at the bar began to intensify, tongues rolling around, hands moving. When Ben reached his hand between her legs, Maggie felt the room spin.

"Excuse me," she said, rising. "I'm not feeling so hot. Be right back."

She tripped over her own feet as she made her way to the women's room. She splashed cold water on her face, and then leaned over the toilet, thinking she might puke. She didn't but the room was still twirling. As she pushed the door open to leave, her other hand reached for the sea glass in her pocket. Ben's face was on the other side of the door. Then it was on top of her, pushing her back in the bathroom, her back pressed up against a baby-changing table.

"Hot. Let's do it in here." His face was back on hers, open mouthed, panting. Her back was pinned, she closed her eyes and tried to regain her balance. Again, she thought she might puke.

"Sorry, I don't think I'm up for it." She wanted to lie down, her knees felt shaky.

He thrust his pelvis on hers and grinded. "Too late, I'm definitely up." He was unzipping his khakis.

"No, really," she said, pushing him away.

His bloodshot eyes made his irises seem as green as a Martian. He closed them and pushed her back against the wall. "Come on," he whispered in her ear, "it will only take a minute."

She slid to the ground. "No. I think I might puke."

She tried to stand up to get to the toilet, but Ben lay on top of her, pulling down his pants. She could hardly see straight, could only focus on the brown stubble starting to come in under his chin. He pulled her pants down past her hips when she pushed herself up on her hands to try to stand up.

"Stop!" she said with as much force as she could muster.

But he pinned her down with his forearm on her chest; he was so strong with his full body weight on her that she could hardly budge. She tried to bite him but her mouth wasn't anywhere near his flesh, and she was simply too tired and drunk to fight more. As he entered her and started pumping away, seemingly oblivious to her, Maggie focused her energy on trying not to puke. And good to his word, it only took a minute—perhaps the longest minute of her life.

"Always good to run into you Maggie," he said, zipping up his khakis while she was still sprawled out on the tile floor. "See you around." And he left.

She stayed there on the floor, touching her Barcelona sea glass still tucked in her pocket. She tried to picture the shade of turquoise that the Mediterranean Sea held when she had picked them up. She envisioned the pieces of a broken soda bottle being slowly caressed by the rhythms of the moving water and sand, softening the rough edges, buffing it into a jewel. Then she sat up and finally vomited in the toilet.

LAURA

SHE COULDN'T BELIEVE it had taken her twenty-five years to realize what must have been obvious to everyone else. She had been the other woman. A home wrecker. The cause for a divorce. The idea of Dan having had a wife seemed so abstract that it wasn't until she actually saw Joy that she was able to see her role. And she didn't like what she saw.

She wanted to hate Joy, this woman who her husband once loved enough to marry. Hate her for her success, for her thinness, for the fact she got to have a daughter. But envisioning Joy's face when she was back home alone in her bed, all she could think was that Joy was the saddest woman she had ever encountered. Then there were the boys, confused and silent. Jacob completely blindsided, angrily storming out the restaurant after Cassie. He wouldn't even accept a ride from them back to his apartment, saying, "I'd rather walk a hundred miles to get to her than ride in your car."

Now she could see that her insistence to not tell their kids about Dan's first marriage wasn't really out of concern for them. Yes, it was true—there were no children, so why confuse the issue for them? And—it was so short, almost like it didn't happen, don't you think? Dan thought they should know. "The fewer secrets in a family, the better," he had said. But he went along with Laura, only saying, "They'll find out later, it always comes out." She now knew that the reason she didn't want them to know that Dan had a first wife was that they would ask the question. Why did you get divorced? The answer made her want to throw up.

So, after one of the longest, most silent hundred miles they had ever driven together, Laura spent the rest of the night packing up the shit that Dan had left behind. She started with his books. The fact that he left his most precious possessions behind showed her that he thought he was coming back. After clearing out the bookshelves she moved on to their walk-in closet. She dumped all of his off-season clothes in large trash bags. While still in the closet, her three sons peeked their heads through the doorway. The fact that they all came together broke her heart a little more.

"Mom, what are you doing?" Jesse asked.

"I'm getting some of your Dad's things together. So he can have them with him."

"But he lives in a hotel, Mom," John said.

Not my problem, she thought, but didn't reply.

"I thought Daddy was coming home soon," little Sam said, his eyes full of un-dropped tears.

I thought so too, she thought, but kept to herself.

"We don't understand why you are so mad at him. This all happened a long time ago, didn't it?" Jesse asked.

Of course they don't understand, how could they? She wasn't sure she did either.

She waved for them to come in. They all sat on the carpeted floor of the closet.

"Yes, it happened a long time ago. But there are a lot of things your dad and I are trying to sort out. It's complicated, in ways that adults have to deal with."

"Can't you work it out with Dad living here?" John asked.

"No. Not right now. I'm sorry. But you need to know how much we both love you boys. This doesn't have anything to do with you guys."

"But what about Jacob? He was so mad." Sam started crying. "Will we see Jacob again?"

She took Sam on her lap and held him tight. "Of course you will see Jacob again. Jacob loves his brothers more than anyone."

"Not more than Cassie," Jesse said.

"There are different kinds of love, boys. Yes, Jacob loves Cassie so much that he wants to marry her. But the family love we have for each other can't be broken, okay?"

"Is Dad included in the family love?" John asked.

And that was the question that she couldn't answer. Not because she was afraid to tell them, but because she honestly didn't know.

JOYCE

CASSIE DIDN'T SHOW for their scheduled run on Sunday morning. She wouldn't answer texts or calls, or the door when Joyce went to her apartment and pounded on it. She could see her car parked under the carport, so she felt certain she was there. But after her knuckles were almost bleeding, she left and went home. Joyce skipped the run and got out her yoga mat, deciding to meditate instead. With pillows propped under her knees, she half kneeled, placed her palms turned up on her thighs and closed her eyes.

She focused on her breathing and asked herself for an intention to focus on when her thoughts drifted. Mercy. That's what came in her head for an intention. She fought back the urge to wonder mercy for whom? She just focused on the inhale, holding it at the top, then the exhale, fully pressing it out.

When her thoughts of Cassie, of Dan, of Laura, and of Jacob came in, she asked them to move on by. She spelled MERCY, like using a finger in the sand, in her mind's eye. Techniques she had learned years ago at a conference she went to in San Francisco. Before she met Andy, when she was trying to nurse her broken heart from Dan. Today the decision seemed to be between meditating and getting drunk. She chose the mat for now, anyway. It was only ten a.m.

In and out with the breathing, she didn't know how long she was there. Beginning to feel the out-of-body experience she was going for, she was interrupted by the tone of her phone indicating a received text. Shit, why didn't she silence it?

Inhale, hold, exhale, release. MERCY.

Plunk, plunk—another text. Or was it just a very long one? Abandoning her mat, she rose to grab her phone. Cassie, finally.

I need some time alone. Please give me that.

And then a second one right after–

I love you.

Joyce responded: Please. We need to talk.

We will talk. Just not now. I need to be alone. You of all people should understand.

It felt like a slap on Joyce's face. How many times in the last year had Joyce told Cassie she needed some time alone? To be patient with her? That she loved her?

She typed: I understand. Run tomorrow?

If anything would get Cassie out the door, it would be a run.

Don't know. I'll get back to you.

And then another: Bye, mom. Love you.

Returning to the mat, she realized the bubble of tranquility had been broken. She stretched out on her back, not concerning herself with the breathing, but just laying Shavasana style. Tomorrow she would connect with Cassie. For now, she would give her some time. She would just liethere until it was time to go to work. She could take the day off, but what would she do? Lieon her mat all day?

Maybe. She felt lethargic, too tired to even get up to go pee. Maybe she could sleep and escape to dreamland. Just last night she replayed when she first met Andy— waiting tables at a pizza joint, she had to go back in the kitchen to beg them to make a pepperoni on the fly; to her horror, she had dropped the first one, right in front of the customers onto the tile floor. There was Andy leaning against the counter in Levi's, a T-shirt, and an apron, smirking before he agreed to with a wink. She wanted to go back to that dream; she wished she could order them up before falling asleep—like setting an alarm. But she had to pee so badly that she just lay there, thinking, when her intention came floating back in. Mercy. And then an image of Laura, pretty and plump in her cardigan sweater.

DAN

FINDING A DECENT place to rent month-to-month seemed almost impossible. Most places simply wouldn't allow anything less than a twelve-month lease. Those that did were in horrible neighborhoods, looked to be infested with cockroaches, or too small to have the boys for an overnight. The thought of taking up semi-permanent residence in the hotel he had been staying at made him want to slit his wrists.

Now he was being shown some houses by a realtor, seeing if he could afford to buy something for himself until Laura took him back. Then he could turn it into a rental. Maybe his salary wouldn't stretch that far—still being responsible for bills at his *real* house—but he had to try. Something had to be done.

He was baffled at Laura's reaction to what he now called the Joy Dinner.

"Why are you so upset with me?" he had asked her. He had dropped Laura and the boys off when they got back into town, at Laura's insistence, but he came back over after the boys went to bed. He incorrectly thought that Laura would calm down before talking alone with her.

"It was *you* who didn't want to tell them about it all along. Maybe we could have prevented something like this from happening."

"Blame me, nice move. Wow, you really have some nerve." She wouldn't even look him in the eye.

"Tell me, what has gotten into you? You knew about Joyce long before we were married. What was it about seeing her tonight that has set you off?" He was used to dealing with her insecurities about other women, admittedly not without merit, given his behavior. But she had had that wild look in her eyes for hours now; this was different.

"No, you tell me something. What did you tell Joy about me after I answered the phone in your office that night?" She finally met his gaze.

"I have no idea what you are talking about. When?" He sat on the couch in the living room. He was so weary— all he wanted to do was fall in bed, preferably with Laura.

"Bullshit, you know the night. The night you told me you had a wife." The intensity of her glare could start a fire.

"I told you, things were already so bad between us. I didn't have to say much." He patted the spot next to him.

"What did you tell her, Dan?" She ignored the invitation to sit.

"I told her it was over. I told her I was in love with someone else. And I was, I am, Laura."

"Did Amber know you were married? Or do you still take off your ring in class?" Laura walked over to the chair furthest from Dan and sat down, arms crossed over her chest.

"Okay, I see what's going on here." The longest night of his life continued. "Please let's go to therapy to work this out."

"Did you tell Amber that your wife wasn't sexually fulfilling you? That she just didn't understand you?"

"Laura, I have been an ass, I will admit that to anyone. All I want is for you to forgive me, so that we can move on together, as a family. I love you." He hadn't been so honest with Laura in years, he only hoped she would believe him.

"I just don't know if that's enough anymore. Seeing Joy made me realize how naive I was, probably still am. Yes, you have been an ass. But, I've been a fool." She stood up, tears filled her eyes.

"Remember, I chose you. Over Joy I chose you, over Amber I chose you. You." He wanted to touch her, to convince her of the sincerity of his words, but stopped himself. Her hostility was palpable.

"Wouldn't it better though, if you didn't have to make the choice?" she asked him and turned to leave.

He didn't respond. She was right of course, but he wanted it so desperately to be different. "Please promise that you will keep our Monday appointment. Don't you think we need to rally right now? Especially for Jacob's sake?"

She just nodded and dismissed him from his own house.

He was standing in a three-bedroom bungalow on Monday morning that had some potential when he received a text from her: Sorry, I just can't. You should go alone. Maybe delve into your pattern with students?

Damn, just when he thought he was back in.

JACOB

HE WAS KICKED out of his own apartment. Just like his dad, he thought bitterly. What was that expression about the sins of the father? He wished he could beat the shit out of his father. He could hardly think straight he was so angry.

It would have been weird enough to find out his dad had been married. He would have been curious about his ex-wife. Was she like Mom? How did you meet? That kind of thing. He would have wanted to know what had happened. Why did you divorce? Did it break your heart? But he didn't have to ask those questions. Cassie told him all about it from behind the closed front door to their apartment after he walked home from the dinner.

"He *cheated* on her," she wailed.

"He's an asshole. I know this. Please let me in."

"The ex-husband who ruined her young life. The example I have been hearing about my whole life for why not to get married in college. It took her a year to recover."

"Cassie, please. He's not a good husband. To my mom either."

"And your mom. She was the reason. Oh my God, I feel sick."

Jacob leaned his back against the door and slid down and sat on the concrete. He was thirsty from the walk and was getting a blister on the back of his right heel. The loafers he had worn to the dinner didn't make great walking shoes. He wanted to reassure his fiancée, say the right thing, but he was so confused himself.

"This is awful. I can't imagine how it must feel for you, with what happened to your dad, wanting to protect your mom."

"Am I adding to my mom's misery?" Her cries were audible through the cheap wood door. "She wouldn't even come back in the room, Jacob."

"I don't know what to say. I love you."

Jacob waited for what seemed too long.

"Well, I love you. It's just that I don't know."

Jacob let his own pent-up tears fall at her hesitation to tell him she loved him. He hung his head between his knees and let out all the frustration and fear that had been building up on his walk there. He hadn't cried so hard since losing the semi-final baseball game in fourth grade.

"Cassie, I found out that my parents have kept a secret from me for my whole life tonight. At least you knew about your mom's marriage. At least your mom and dad had a happy marriage. My parents have been *lying* to me. Their relationship *sucks*. How do you think I feel?"

"Oh, Jacob." He imagined her touching the door, reaching out for him. He listened to hear the door click open but it was silent. "I'm so sorry. But I need to think of my mom right now. She doesn't have anyone else."

"Bullshit. She has Maggie, she has everyone at work. It's not fair. I didn't do anything wrong." He immediately wished he could take back his angry defensive tone, but it was too late.

"Please go stay with Ryan tonight. I need to be alone."

So he took off his shoes and socks and started walking. He wouldn't get another blister but he might step on glass or a nail on the way to Ryan's. *Good*, he thought. He felt raindrops fall from what had appeared to be a cloudless sky. *Perfect*, he thought, not bothering to shield himself, *maybe I'll get hit by lightning*. He looked like a junkie or something, shuffling down the sidewalk with no shoes on in the rain, crying. He didn't care.

He got his phone out of his pocket and punched in a number. It went straight to voicemail. "Call me back, you fucking coward."

MAGGIE

IT WAS CRAZY how much she had to pee these days. And how tired she was. She had no idea that hormones could have such a transformative effect on her body. She wasn't even showing yet. She shuddered to think what it would be like with a huge belly. At least she hadn't felt sick at all. Joyce had been violently ill with morning sickness for months with Cassie. Maggie couldn't see how she could possibly work if she felt that way—the demands of the kitchen were exhausting enough. She could picture Andy's face, tired at the end of a night, when he used to tell her, "Kitchen work is for the young." How right he was.

She and Joyce passed in the hall, their first encounter since Saturday night.

"Any lunch specials?" Joyce asked her, all business.

"Same as yesterday," Maggie answered. "We'll change it tomorrow."

She was waiting for an apology, but Joyce just walked off, holding her clipboard with the schedule on it.

She first noticed the spotting when she was in the

bathroom before the lunch shift. Her panties were wet with a small spot of pink blood. Her heart beat in her ears as she sat on the toilet frozen. Calm down, take a breath, she told herself, yet she had a hard time moving. She dabbed with more toilet paper—no more pink. Go back to work, cook lunch, and then deal with this. When she didn't know what to do, she inevitably fell back to work. She knew what needed to be done there. She grabbed a liner from a box kept below the sink, put it on top of the stain, and returned to the kitchen.

Lunch shift was slow, which was much worse than being busy. With incoming tickets flying off the kitchen printer, all she could think about was keeping up. But when minutes passed in between orders she had too much time to brood.

"Nice job holding the wall up, Jones. You know what they say. If there's time to lean, there's time to clean." She was working with a bunch of chumps.

Pedro was off for the week visiting relatives in Mexico City, which contributed to her emotional imbalance. "I want you to come with me. Meet my people." But she begged off, too much work, Joyce needed her, blah, blah, blah. She wished she had gone after all.

Incoming orders having dwindled to a trickle, she grabbed her phone and locked herself back in the bathroom. Her liner was clean. She opened her browser and typed in "spotting pregnant." She scanned the results—*common, especially during first trimester, no cause for alarm, see your doctor, rule out miscarriage.*

It had always been enough for Maggie to be an aunt. She was never one of those girls who wrote down their favorite baby names in their diaries like her friends in grade school. She was not emotionally tortured over not having had children, even when she turned forty. In fact, she had spent all of her adult life trying to prevent pregnancy. So it came as a bit of shock to realize how important this baby was to her now. The fact that she was referring to her unborn child as a baby was a testament to that. In the past she would have been the first person to point out that it was actually an embryo. Feeling devastated by the thought she could be losing her baby, she was almost as sad at the fact that she was still irate with the one person she wanted to reach out to.

CASSIE

WHEN HER MOM texted her about the run, she almost wrote back to forget about the whole marathon training. But some fresh air would probably do her some good. She had skipped class for the past two days and hadn't left her apartment.

Can we meet at your place? Joyce had texted. They never met there.

Why?

I want to talk.

Let's talk while running.

Just for a few minutes. Be there soon.

Now her mom wanted to come over. All the times she wished she would just stop by, they could have easy-going chitchats about stupid stuff like nail polish and eat ice cream directly from the container. She changed her clothes and pulled her hair back into a ponytail. She normally would have worn one of Jacob's ball caps since it looked sunny, but she couldn't bring herself to. Her mom arrived as she was lacing up her shoes.

"Where's Jacob?" Joyce asked as she sat down on the couch.

"He's not here."

"Obviously. Listen, I know he lives here, okay?"

"He's staying at his friend Ryan's place."

"About Saturday night," Joyce began. "I'm sorry I vanished."

"It must have been quite a shock for you to see them."

"What did they say? What happened exactly?"

Cassie almost laughed—her mom was actually trying to pump her for information, to find out what she knew.

"Gosh, Mom, what do you think happened?"

"Honey, I don't know. That's why I'm asking."

Cassie let out a huge sigh. "Dan told us that he was your first husband."

"Oh God, how awful, with all the boys and Laura there?"

"Yes, the whole crowd was gathered."

"Did he say anything else?"

"No, that was plenty. None of the boys even knew he

had been married before. I just got up and left. Can we run now?"

"No, not yet. I'm so sorry I wasn't there. It was. . . difficult. . . coming face to face with him, even after all these years. I should have dealt with it better. I'm sorry it came out like this. It's all such a shock, with Jacob and all."

"Well, I want you to know that I think you're right after all. About waiting. To get married, that is."

"Oh, Cassie, what do you mean?"

"I'm going to ask Jacob to move out. This is all too much."

"Honey, yes, it's too much, I agree. But slow down. Have you even talked to Jacob? He must be having a hard time with all of this."

"Why should we talk about it? How can I possibly marry him now?" Cassie fell into the couch and put her head in her hands. "Why does it feel like I've been sleeping with my brother or something?" Her body was shaking.

Joyce scooted next to her, drew her in close, being a cradle rocking her back and forth. Cassie hadn't let her mom hold her like this in many years. It felt safe.

"Honey, this too shall pass. This too shall pass."

Cassie looked up. "How could we possibly have a wedding? Would you be able to sit next to them? After what he did to you? Would you think of Dan every time you saw Jacob?"

"I'm a big girl. This is about you, not me."

"But you don't have anyone to look out for you anymore. How could I possibly ask you to be okay with this?"

"I can look after myself, honey, it's not your job. I'm okay, really. You've got to live your life, that's what your dad would want."

But Cassie didn't believe her. Her mom hadn't been okay since the day she had found her daddy dead in the shower. She doubted her daddy would even recognize the shell that her mom had become.

Cassie sat up and wiped her face with her hands. "I'll live my life if you live yours."

Joyce just closed her eyes, still and silent.

"Oh, and let's forget about the marathon. I'm relieving you from your obligation." And she put on her headphones and went out the door, leaving her mom on the couch alone.

LAURA

LAURA THOUGHT THAT she should get a job, at least something part time, to contribute to the increased expenses of paying for two houses. They might have to cut out some of the boys' sports activities if something didn't change. She remembered something her mom said to her in college. Why get a job when you can get a husband? Maybe the worst advice she had ever heard.

She wanted to see if she was good at anything, if she was valuable enough to be hired by someone. But looking at available work online turned out to be very discouraging. Even with her undergraduate Humanities degree, she really wasn't qualified to do anything that seemed professional. Part-time and flexible hours proved to be equally elusive. Realistic options were limited. There was always retail, but the thought of running into the mothers of her kids' friends felt horrifying. And she would probably spend more than she would end up making, even with the employee discount. Those sale racks were just too tempting.

Many listings for childcare workers existed, but she had done her time with that. The thought of working in a preschool helping kids on the potty made her want to cry. There was temporary work, being sent to offices and such for a limited time, but the pay was awful. And then there was restaurant work—waiting tables and bartending being one of the best part-time, flexible hourly wages you could find. Maybe Joy would give her a job. Joyce.

Her neighbor, Rhonda, sat at her kitchen table with her, comparing Weight Watchers tips. "What's your dream job?"

"I don't even know anymore. I've haven't thought about it in years."

"Well, what used to be your dream job?"

She was reluctant to tell her. She thought she would sound like a moron, or at least delusional.

"Come on, Laura. I won't tell anyone. I'll go ahead and tell you mine. I've always wanted to have my own dog grooming business. I know, I know, all the hair and disagreeable customers—Mike thinks it's so stupid. But I love dogs, and I love making them pretty." She stopped to smile at Laura. "See, that wasn't so hard."

"It's not stupid at all. You would be great at that."

"Now, your turn."

"Well, my dad was a philosophy professor. I guess I

always imagined that I would teach at the collegiate level." She shook her head ruefully. "Instead I just married a professor. Just like my mother did. Pretty pathetic, huh?"

"Not pathetic. You have raised, *are* raising, fantastic, well-adjusted kids. But it may be the dawn of a new day for you," she said smiling. "I just had a lightning bolt great idea. Go back to graduate school. Become that teacher."

Laura laughed. "That is the opposite of a job. More unpaid work, great." But her pulse quickened at the thought.

"Don't you get free tuition as part of Dan's perks?"

"Yes," she hesitated. "Provided we stay together, of course."

"Shit, stay together for the free tuition. That's an amazing opportunity. Maybe you could get a work-study job or something on campus to actually bring in a check."

"I don't know . . ."

"Well, if you are going to reject the best idea I've had this year, I'm going to take off." Rhonda gathered her calorie counters and other worksheets from the table.

"Hey, Rhonda, thanks. Really."

"Thanks for giving me the weight loss pep talk." She walked toward the door and then turned around. "Now don't be such a chicken shit. Okay?"

"I'll try. See you at the meeting tomorrow."

Laura sat in front of her computer and closed the browser with the job listings. Starting a fresh search, she typed in "master of humanities."

JOYCE

HOLED UP IN her office with the door locked, Joyce gazed at her sketch, seemingly unable to continue. She completed the bed with the pile of her clothes, the hangers still on. The contents from the short hanging rod in the closet—her blouses and sweaters that required being hung to keep their shape—neatly stacked on the bed. She had drawn it with a charcoal pencil then filled in some color for the clothes and bedspread. She finished the wood open door with its shiny brass knob. But she was unable to get started on the inside of the closet.

Her therapist, Amy, asked her every week now, "How is your drawing coming?" She regretted telling her that she had started it. She hadn't even been to see her since the Dan fiasco. But for the first time since starting therapy she was actually looking forward to her next appointment. She needed to unburden herself. Maybe it was because she and Maggie hadn't been talking. These spats had been going on their whole lives, at their worst when their mother was dying. They always made up eventually, but this time Joyce felt Maggie's absence more acutely. Just when Joyce was going to apologize to her, Maggie took a sick day. She decided to stop by her place later to check on her.

Focus on the carpet first and then work your way up, she told herself in order to start drawing the inside of the closet. Just as she started on the tan shag she heard a knock on her door.

"Mrs. Becker, it's Jacob. Can I talk to you please?"

"Sure, Jacob. Give me a sec." She swiftly locked the pad up and opened the door. Jacob stared at her, eyes red, stubble on his chin. "Come in. Can I get you anything? Coffee, soda, or maybe a drink?" She had never seen him look so terrible.

"No, thank you. I just need to talk." He stood awkwardly, holding his hands together in front of him. "She won't see me. She won't even talk to me. She wants me to move out. I don't know what to do."

"Come, sit down. I need coffee for myself; I'll bring you a cup. Do you take anything in it?"

"No, just black. Thank you, Mrs. Becker."

When she returned with the coffee, Jacob was looking at the photos she kept in frames on her windowsill. Joyce and Andy grinning with a twenty-dollar bill from their first day in business. A black and white of Joyce and Maggie as children in a sandbox. Andy holding a baby Cassie, all swaddled up like a bean. Cassie, Andy, and Joyce on Cassie's college graduation.

They sat down with their coffee.

"I don't know what to say. This is all so unexpected, so complicated," Joyce said.

"I came because I wanted to apologize." He took a drink of coffee.

"Apologize for what? You didn't do anything."

"Apologize for my father. For what happened, what he did to you." Tears rolled from his red-rimmed eyes. "I didn't even know about any of it."

"Oh no, it's not your fault. Don't apologize for him." She resisted the urge to give him a hug.

"Someone needs to. He's been such a jerk, not just to you but also to my mom. I don't want to be anything like him. And if I lose Cassie because of him. . ." He wiped his eyes with his fists. "So please, I'm sorry. Okay?"

His vulnerability touched her. He really didn't seem like his dad. Dan always exuded such a confident, almost arrogant persona. And while he looked more like his mother, Joyce could see Dan in him. The way his eyes crinkled in certain expressions, the patterns of his voice, the way he held the coffee cup.

"Okay," she answered as he rose to leave.

"Thank you for the coffee. Where should I put the cup?" he asked.

"Just leave it," she told him, and walked up to him and gave him a hug. Still holding him, she whispered in his ear, "It's going to be okay. Everything is going to be okay." She questioned herself afterwards—for whose benefit did she really say those words?

DAN

HE DID END up going to the therapy appointment without his wife. He even spilled his guts to the guy in corduroy pants and a brown sweater. Phil was his name, recommended by his neighbor Mike. At least Mike and Rhonda had been able to stay together. So far, anyway. But spilling his guts to Phil didn't get him back into his house, or stop the hostile conversations with Jacob, which usually ended with his son telling him that he was ruining his life before hanging up on him.

The only person who could tolerate being around him these days was his youngest son, Sam, who didn't seem to understand what was going on with everyone else. Then there were his students. Normally he would engage in activities outside the classroom with them—poetry readings, seminars, and such—but not this semester. He was determined not to get in another of what he called his "entanglements" this year. At least Phil helped him look at strategies to avoid that. One of them was severely limiting his office hours and encouraging e-mail communication, which he normally hated. But being in his small office with some of the girls alone, some of these *students* alone, he corrected himself, was a sure way to a future problem.

So he was surprised when, as he was eating lentil soup from a to-go container from behind his desk, he heard a knock on his door. It was not office hours, in fact he didn't have any at all that day. Occasionally someone would wander by lost, looking for someone else's office. Otherwise he never had visitors. The interruption made him a little irritated, thinking that it was a student who was ignoring his explicit instructions. "Come in."

Joy pushed open the door. His irritation was quickly replaced with surprise.

"Sorry to barge in on you without any warning," she said, still standing in the doorway. She was wearing a pair of jeans with a green T-shirt, her dark hair pulled back, and holding a cup of coffee. She didn't look like she did when they were together, (did he?), but she looked good, maybe better even. She had lost that baby face—he saw shadows of her mother, Ann, in how she gazed at him, standing there.

"Hi, come in. Please." He rose to greet her but neither of them could figure out what to do. Shake hands? Wave? Hug?

So they just stood there.

"Would you like to sit down?"

"Yes, thank you," she said, lowering herself into a chair. She looked really thin.

"I'm glad you came. I've wanted to talk to you since Saturday but was unsure how to go about it." These words were true. It was also true that he was scared to see Joy again. Scared at having to face how he had conducted himself with her all those years ago; scared at how she might treat him now; scared that he might find himself drawn to her again.

"Jacob came to see me. He's really hurting."

"I know. This has been enormously difficult for him. I've tried talking with him, but he is so angry."

"He came to me to apologize for you." She finished her cup of coffee and threw it in his wastebasket. "Do you still keep a pack of cigarettes hidden in here somewhere?"

Dan laughed. "No, I had to give up my one-a-day habit when smoking was banished from campus."

"I quit ages ago, too. But the occasional. . . I'm just really nervous."

Dan had always liked her candor; she was willing to say things that other women tried to hide. "The occasional for me has become scotch. I just wish I could say it was really only occasionally." He pulled out a bottle of McCallan 12 year from his bottom drawer and fished out two cups. He poured a splash into each and handed her one.

"Jacob is a good man. I'm sure you know that, but I can see why Cassie fell in love with him."

"His mother's influence I'm sure."

"No, really. You should be proud of him. I'm sure you are."

"Yes. It makes the wrath he has toward me now all the more painful."

"It broke my heart when he said he wanted to apologize for you. And it made me wonder if I really have forgiven you." She took a large gulp of the scotch. She looked him in the eye. "Isn't that crazy? After all these years? After finding the love of my life after we split?" She finished her drink. He took his as a shot. He poured another.

"And?"

"And what?"

"And, have you forgiven me?" He held his breath for the answer. He would be willing to beg for her forgiveness now if it would benefit his son. If it could ease his conscience. If it could relieve the feeling of having a brick on his chest at all the time trying to pin him down.

"I decided it didn't matter. What's done is done, we've both moved on. That's enough for me."

"I'm going to record that as forgiveness extended," he said.

"You would." She smiled. When she smiled she was so pretty, she had this incredibly wide mouth with large white teeth. But even with the big smile, sadness clung to her eyes.

"I'm sorry about your husband. That's just too young." She nodded. "And your mother. Ann was a special woman."

"I'm sorry to hear you and Laura are having problems." She seemed like she really meant it.

"I'm sorry your first husband was such a jerk." He held his hands out, palms lifted.

"I'm sorry your son hates you." She smiled again.

"I'm sorry you are drinking single malt scotch out of a coffee cup."

"I'm sorry you're still teaching here."

"I'm sorry you're not a famous artist. I thought you would be." He remembered the easel she had set up in their kitchen.

"I give up. There is nothing else that I can find about your life to be sorry about. But you know what? I'm not sorry about not being an artist. Life's been really good to me. Well, until recently."

"I'm glad. Really." He realized that he had rarely thought of her over the years. Maybe a student's sharp wit would remind him of her in passing, but he never really considered what she might be doing with her life.

"I thought of another," he said. "I'm sorry I took you for granted. I'm sorry I acted like your feelings didn't matter."

She just looked at him for a moment. "Okay, forgiveness extended."

"Can I get that recorded for Jacob's benefit?"

She sighed loudly. "Oh my, in a million years I would have never. . ."

"Guessed?"

"Guessed, yes. Guessed that this would be where we would end up. Drinking scotch from a coffee cup, trying to seek the best interests of our kids. Who happen to love each other."

Dan was beginning to feel loose, relaxed from the

scotch. It was a feeling that lately had been a solitary one, confined to his hotel room with his books. The fact that he was with another person right now, much less Joy, was exhilarating.

"Why can't love win?" he asked with all seriousness.

He watched her physically bristle at the question and then deflate.

"I wish I knew," she answered. "It didn't win for me when I wanted you to love me."

"I'm sorry. Really, I am. I don't think I have been truly sorry until right now."

They just sat in silence.

"I really should go, I'll do what I can with Jacob." Joyce stood up and took a step to the door, then turned back, like she had a question.

But instead of asking a question, she placed her hands on the armrests of his chair. She leaned over slowly toward him, and he knew she was going to kiss him. He relaxed in his chair—waiting for it—when her lips landed on his. He tried not to be greedy, but it felt too good, so strangely familiar that he didn't even try to resist. He released it all into the kiss, surrendered his mouth, then his tongue. His hands reached for her waist, it was so small, then plunged under her shirt. He started reaching up when she pulled away.

"Don't go. Please Joy, stay." But she was walking toward the door.

"It's Joyce," she said over her shoulder. "I'm not going to be Joy for you."

Then she walked out the door.

JACOB

HE HAD PARKED his car in the restaurant parking lot, thinking that Cassie might show up there. Her car wasn't at the apartment and she wasn't in class. He needed to lay eyes on her, even if she didn't want to talk. The distance she was insisting on from him was taking a toll. He couldn't sleep, it was hard to concentrate on his studies, food held no interest for him; he just wanted her. To smell her hair, to hold her. He sat in his car, just waiting, not even listening to music. He leaned his head back on the headrest and wasn't aware that he had fallen asleep until a knock on his window jolted him awake. He wiped the drool from his cheek as he looked up.

"What are you doing in there?" Maggie's face was on the other side of the window, clenched in concern.

He rolled down the window. "Oh hi, Mags. I thought Cassie might stop by. I need to see her."

"It's three o'clock in the afternoon and you are sleeping in your car? You look like shit, Jacob. Come in, let me make something for you."

"It's okay, I can just wait here. You're probably trying to work."

"I was just going to go home and get something, but it can wait. This is my down time before dinner. Come on." She opened his door.

The bowl of pasta she set before him looked delicious—chunks of seared mushrooms and Italian sausage, some sort of small noodle he didn't know that name of, Parmesan cheese covering everything. He hadn't realized he was hungry until he saw it. He realized he couldn't remember when he had last eaten.

"Hope you don't mind leftovers," she said as they leaned against the counter. "Do you want to sit down?"

Jacob shook his head, his mouth full of pasta.

"After the meal I think you should consider a shower, buddy."

He touched his hair—it felt greasy. He still hadn't shaven. He had worn the same outfit for a couple days now.

"Thanks for doing this. I really appreciate it, I do. There isn't anyone I can talk to right now who understands what is going on."

"It's easy to be nice to you, Jacob."

"Mags, can I ask you something?"

"Sure."

"What was my dad like? When you first knew him? When he was with Joyce?"

"Ah, yes, your dad. You know, I was still in high school when I first met Dan. I thought he was the hottest guy I had ever laid eyes on. He had just started graduate school, he's a couple years older than Joyce, I think. Dashing, that's what I thought of him. And he had this smarty-pants thing going on too." She smiled at him. "It was such a long time ago."

"Did he love her?"

"Yes, they were in love, I never doubted that. They had this banter they did, sort of a sarcastic teasing that was pretty adorable. When they got married in my mom's backyard, we all assumed it would be forever."

"So, what happened then?"

She looked at him in the way that Jacob looked at his little brother Sam when he failed to understand something simple. "What happened is what often happens. He fell in love with someone else."

"With my mom?"

"Yes, with your mom. But that's your dad's story, you

should ask him."

"Does love ever last?" he asked with tears in his eyes.

"I hope so," she answered. "Your parents' marriage lasted."

"Not a very good example, I'm afraid," he said, finishing his pasta.

"I wish I had a better one for you, I've never been married."

"Joyce and Andy's love lasted, until he died. Right?" he asked.

"Yes, it did. But I don't think there's a straight line for going the long haul with someone."

"I really want to try with Cassie." He willed himself not to cry again. He had to try to keep it together.

"You and Cassie shared your engagement secret with me. Can I tell you something? Something I haven't told Cassie or even Joyce yet?"

"Yes, of course, what is it?" He looked concerned.

"I thought I had a miscarriage yesterday. Oh yeah, I'm pregnant, I should have said that first."

"Oh, Mags, you're pregnant? Wow, congratulations."

"I thought I lost the baby. The baby that I didn't even know I wanted to have. But I didn't, just normal spotting stuff."

"I'm so glad. You are going to be an awesome mom."

"So I've been thinking about my future, our future, and I realized I really want to make it work with Pedro as a family. I really want this. That actually surprised me."

"I'm so happy for you. Thank you for telling me—it's the first time I've felt good in days now."

"But you know what else I realized? That I may have to fight for it. That it may not be easy or comfortable, but that I want it anyway. Do you know what I'm saying?"

"No, not really."

"What I am saying is that what's true for me, may also be true for you. You may have to fight for what you want."

He sat in silence, absorbing what she said and set his empty bowl on the counter. Then he raised his fists in a boxer pose. "I may have to fight for it, yes." He did a little foot-work and made some jabs into the air.

"Easy, Rocky." Maggie laughed. "First, go take a shower and put on some deodorant. Then go win your girl back."

CASSIE

SHE THOUGHT THAT if she went to the restaurant at a peak time, say about seven p.m., she could see her mom and Maggie without having to stay too long. They would be too busy, she knew from experience, to sit down and have a heart-to-heart, which was exactly what she was hoping to avoid.

Unfortunately, they were still waiting for the dinner rush when she showed up. She stopped in the kitchen first, hoping to start with an easy and light conversation with her aunt. But the expression on Maggie's face was concern, her mouth turned down.

"There you are. Girl, do I need to give you a lecture about returning texts? I thought you had been kidnapped."

"You really should stop watching so much *Law & Order*. Makes you paranoid."

"And now you want me to cut back on my favorite way to decompress after work?"

"I know, I know, you've already basically got your law degree from watching the show. I don't know why I'm

171

bothering with this law school nonsense."

Maggie smiled at her—this was better. "Can you hang around? Let's have a drink after the rush. Talk a bit." Three tickets came popping out of the kitchen printer, distracting Maggie.

"Sorry, gotta run. The amount of reading this semester is atrocious." Cassie blew her a kiss. "Love you."

She found her mom behind the point-of-sales terminal, voiding an item for a server.

"We can't just comp everything that you screw up, Sarah. Please be more careful with entering your orders," she told a new server standing next to her. "Hi, honey." Her face brightened when she saw Cassie.

She handed the revised ticket to the server and they walked off to the bar.

"I should be able to get away soon. Do you want to go get ice cream or something?" Her mom had been using this technique for years now to get in the same car with her.

"Maybe next time, I have a ton of work I've been neglecting." She knew that her mom would never recommend that she blow off her responsibilities. "Soon though, I just wanted to say hi. Tell you I'm okay."

"Thanks, I've been thinking about you a lot. And before you run off, there's something I want to tell you."

Cassie braced herself, not wanting to talk about Jacob with her right now. "What?"

"I think we should run the marathon in San Diego. No matter what else is going on, I want to run it with you. Okay?"

"Ok, Mom. I'd like that." She meant it—her runs felt lonely lately.

"And there's something else. Let's take the ashes with us. What do you think?"

Caught off guard completely, she felt like she might start crying. So she just nodded, gave her mom a hug, and left without saying a word.

CASSIE

CASSIE KNEW SOMETHING was wrong when she received a text from her mom wondering if she happened to be with her dad. It was weird for her mom to be looking for him; they were almost always together at work. She would only ask Cassie if she were really worried, despite the attempt at seeming casual in the text. Leaving her stack of books at her desk in her tiny, sparse apartment, she tried to stay calm. As Cassie drove over to their house—the house she had spent much of her childhood in—the angle of the twilight sun assaulted her eyes, the visor on the windshield failed to cover any of its blaze. Almost blinded by the light, she noticed a fire engine and an emergency vehicle as she passed them. *The sirens aren't blaring*, nevertheless, her heart beat wildly.

Both of her parents' cars were parked in the driveway. *Oh good, she found him. Everything's okay,* she thought as pulled in to park behind her mom's car. The front door was wide open, she pulled it shut behind her as she shouted, "Hello! I can't believe you guys aren't at work." She stopped to listen for a response, wondering if they were in the kitchen or the other side of the house where their bedroom was. She noticed her mom's suitcase in the hallway. Hearing nothing, she walked to the kitchen. Empty, impeccably clean, one dirty coffee mug sitting in the sink.

Walking back to the bedroom, she yelled, "Want to go out to dinner since you're off? I'm coming back there, get yourself decent if you need to." She never wanted to walk in on them again; the trauma of catching them in the act when she was fifteen was awful. But the bedroom door was open, and when she peeked in the doorway it was empty inside. It all looked normal expect for a big pile of clothes on hangers laid out on the bed. A blue silk tank was on top, one that she had her eye on for borrowing; she would swipe it on her way out. She went to examine the pile—all her mom's blouses and shirts—why were they there? It looked like she was packing them to move them or something. Where were her parents anyway?

She turned to check in the bathroom. There was water all over the floor, footprints tracked through in all directions. Towels were balled around the shower, smeared with something red. Blood?

Cassie suddenly felt afraid, the quiet was strangely deafening. She reached for her phone, with shaking hands located it at the bottom of her purse. She called her dad's number first, heard it ring once in the bedroom before going to voicemail. She hung up and dialed her mom. It rang four times before her mom's voice came on the line.

"Cassie?" she whispered.

"Where are you?" she asked.

"I'll call you later," her mom said, so quietly she could barely hear.

"What's going on? Why aren't you guys at work?"

"I can't talk now."

"Why not? Where's Dad?"

"Don't come over."

"I'm already here, in the bathroom. Where are you?" All Cassie could hear from the other end of the line was silence, followed by gasping breaths. "Mom?"

She walked out of the bathroom, phone to her ear, back in the bedroom, looking around for someone. She heard a click and her phone showed that the called ended. She sat down on her parents' bed, next to the pile of clothes, listening—for anything, evidence that someone was in the house. *Did someone have Mom? What were the red smeared towels in the bathroom? Where's Daddy?*

She had dialed the 9 for 911 when the door to the closet

opened from the inside. She looked around, panicked, to find something she could defend herself with. She was grabbing a wire hanger when her mom emerged. Her hair was wet, pasted to the sides of her face, mascara smeared down to her cheeks. In fact, all of her clothes appeared to be wet—she looked as if she had walked through a hurricane. She just stood there, arms at her sides, staring at Cassie.

"Mom, what is going on? I am really freaked out."

Joyce sat next to her on the bed.

"Why are you wet?"

No answer.

"Why are your clothes here on the bed?"

More silence.

"Where's Daddy?" That question seemed to jolt her.

Her mom turned to her. "I need to tell you something. Something really hard to say. Okay?"

Cassie nodded her head.

"I came home and found Daddy dead."

No. No. No. Not that.

"Cassie? Did you hear me?"

"Yes, I heard you," she answered. *This isn't possible, this is a riddle, a test, a problem to figure out.*

"Where was he?" she asked. *This isn't true.*

"In the shower."

"He was dead in the shower?" *Impossible, he is the strongest man alive.*

"Yes."

"That's why you're wet?" *My daddy couldn't be dead in the shower.*

"The shower was running and I went in to get him," her mom answered.

"How could he have died in the shower?" *What is real?*

"I don't know, they thought maybe a heart attack."

"Why was there blood on the towels?" *I am going to be a lawyer, I will fix this.*

"There was no blood, honey, I don't know what you're talking about."

She ran into the bathroom, almost falling on the wet tile, grabbed the wet towels streaked with red, and held them before her mom like an offering. "This blood, Mom."

Her mom rose and took the towels from her. "That's not blood, it's lipstick."

"Bullshit," Cassie snapped. "You don't wear red lipstick." *My mom is lying to me.*

"I wore it to dress up, to see your dad. I've been in Florida, remember?"

"Did someone hurt him?" *My daddy is not dead.*

"No, nothing like that."

"Why were you in the closet?" *My mom is lying to me.*

"I wanted to be alone." Her mom's shoulders started shaking before she saw the tears pour out. She had only seen her mom cry once before in her life, when she had backed into another car and broken the windshield of their car. Seeing her break down caused her own interior to collapse. Holding her elbows tight against her body, she wailed, "Where is he? Where did they take him?"

Her mom put her arms around her. "He's just gone, honey."

And even though Cassie was crying at the thought she was also thinking, *impossible.*

LAURA

JACOB FINALLY PICKED up the phone when she called again and apologized for how she found out about the engagement. He added with confidence, "I'm going to win her back." Maybe he would. When he promised to come to John's game over the weekend, she was so relieved that maybe they could get things back to normal. Whatever normal was these days.

She went online to cancel her Weight Watchers order. Her trainer, Thomas, had suggested a different program through his gym, one that he would personally supervise, he told her, leaning in a bit too close. She should have said no. She had actually lost some weight on her current plan—but he smelled so good (Ivory soap?), he looked so strong.

She opened her journal and started a new list by writing "Dan comes home" on the top of a fresh page. She first wrote "good for family/boys happy," then "financially better." She chewed on the pencil eraser. "easier if I go back to school/help with boys." And with some reluctance, she wrote the final item, "miss him/less lonely."

On the empty part of the page she wrote and underlined, "Divorce Dan." First she wrote the question: "will he ever change?" She couldn't come up with another item—that was the only reason to divorce Dan she could think of. It was also a question without an answer. He was so sorry *now,* but how would it be when he was secure, back at home. She thought of something else to add to the divorce list, "punish Dan." What she also wondered, but didn't write down was— Punish the boys? Punish me?

She peeked in the doorways of the boys, sleeping sprawled out and snoring in their respective bedrooms. It was painfully quiet. Maybe she should get a dog, the boys would love that. The last time she confessed that another baby would be nice, Rhonda had told her, "Not a baby, Laura, get a pet. A high maintenance pet, then you can take it back if it doesn't work out. At least if you are going to touch someone else's shit, with a dog they are always happy to see you." She knew she was too old for another baby. But the thought of becoming one of those women who didn't have a man around and started treating their dog like a child made her shudder. Shoot me if I ever push a dog around in a stroller, she had told Dan once, when on an evening walk they passed a woman with her rat-like dog riding in style.

Sleep proved to be elusive the bed was far too big for one person. She stretched out on her back, trying to enjoy all the room available to her. But instead of drifting off, her mind wandered to the night in the kitchen with Dan. Then the image of her trainer Thomas spotting her with the squat bar, standing right behind her, his body touching hers.

And because she needed the relief, needed to get some sleep, needed the release; she reached her hand between her legs and gave herself some.

MAGGIE

HER SISTER STOOD in front of her, holding a yellow legal pad and pen. "Peter said we're out of the halibut?"

"Yes, but we're prepping it now. Eighty-six it in the computer, but I'll let you know when it's back up. Shouldn't be long." It had been like this for days now, all business.

Joyce lowered her pad and found Maggie's gaze. "I wanted to tell you I'm sorry. I've been a real asshole. You were right, I've been completely self-absorbed."

Maggie paused and smiled and put her arm around her shoulder. "It's okay. What a bombshell dropped. This is a crazy, crazy world isn't it?"

"I've missed you," Joyce told her.

"Ready for another bombshell?" she asked, turning to face her directly.

"Oh God, I don't think so. What is it?" Joyce stiffened.

"I'm going to have a baby. Next summer." She pointed

at her belly. "I'm knocked up." Then she burst into a smile. "I've missed you too."

"*What*? That was not what I was expecting. Oh, Maggie. . ."

"Aren't you happy for me? For Pedro and me? Please say something else."

"I'm so happy for you. This is the best news I could think of." Joyce took her in her arms and hugged her.

"Oh good," Maggie said, wiping tears from her eyes. "These hormones are killing me. I'm so stinking emotional, I hate it."

"I kind of like it actually, seeing my tough-girl little sister in tears occasionally."

"Listen, how is the situation with Cassie? I've barely talked to her, but I did spend some time with Jacob."

"She's hardly talked to me either, but this has been tough on her. She's talking like she's going to break up with him. She somehow thinks that she would be protecting me by doing that."

"You might have to give her permission."

"What do you mean, give her permission for what?"

"With how you've been the last year, she's just worried about you, doesn't want to contribute to your pain.

From my view, it's easy to see—I feel the same way."

"Permission for what, though?"

"You might have to tell her it's okay for her to love Jacob. She may need to hear you say that she can marry him."

Joyce brushed her hand at the thought. "Cassie is an adult. She's always been so headstrong and makes up her own mind. I'm not buying it."

"I'm not trying to sell it, but just think about it. You know how it feels to want to spare your mom pain." It was easy to remember their own mother's suffering.

"Ready for bombshell number three?" Joyce asked her.

"You're pregnant too? You won the lottery? You got a neck tattoo that you're covering up with your sweater?"

Joyce laughed. "No, but close. I kissed Dan. In his office."

"Oh. My. God."

"I know, it wasn't part of my plan, really."

"Well. . . how was it?"

"Come on, what is this? We're not teenagers anymore."

"Okay, must have been lousy then."

"No, it was actually kind of magical in a sort of surreal way."

"A kiss. . . very interesting. I would have guessed a slap or a punch."

"And then I walked away. I left him there."

"Some kind of metaphor there? You should ask Dan—he's the literature guy."

"It was spontaneous, I don't even know why I did it."

"Oh boy, you are entering some unchartered waters here. Be careful."

"Don't be silly, it was just a brief moment of regression from being around him again. I don't. . ."

Will, a server, approached them. "Excuse me, sorry to bust in here. A customer just told me there's some poop on the floor in the women's rest room."

"Some poop?" Maggie asked, eyebrows lifted.

"Yes, her words, some poop," he said, blushing.

"Thanks, Will, I'll take care of it." Joyce turned to Maggie. "Isn't having a restaurant glamorous?"

"Find me later, okay?" Maggie asked.

"Sure. And please, not a word of what I told you to

anyone. Not even dimples."

Maggie turned an imaginary key to lock her mouth.

JACOB

STUDY BUDDY TODAY? he had texted Cassie, using the expression he said over a year ago when he wanted to hang out with her. He added: Ryan picks his nose when he is reading and thinks no one is watching. I don't think I can take it anymore.

Okay, she answered back immediately.

Meet at the library at three?

Yes.

Thinking of Maggie's advice, he took another shower, shaved, and applied extra deodorant. He even gargled with mouthwash and put on his favorite T-shirt. During the walk to the library, the changing leaves seemed illuminated from within—glowing gold, simmering crimson. Fall was his favorite season, a welcome reprieve from the unrelenting heat and humidity of the typical Oklahoma summer.

He stopped to pick up a leaf that caught his eye (maple?) that was vibrant yellow on one side, fading into a lush coral on the other side. Just like a sunset. Which made him think of his wedding. Stuffing the leaf in his pocket, he rushed to the library. And there she was, sitting at the table where they first met, close to the window on the second floor. She hadn't opened a book yet; it looked as if she had just arrived.

She smiled when she saw him. "Hey there, study buddy."

"Hey there, beautiful." Something in the way she held herself, protected and small, prevented him from holding her close to him like he wanted to. He sat down in front of her at the table, dropping his book bag off to the side.

"I've missed you," he said. He laid the leaf in front of her.

"I've missed you too," she said, pulling her hair behind her ears and then picking up the miniature sunset in her hands.

"I want to come home," he said.

"I think you should."

"Oh, thank God, Cassie, this has been the worst week of my life."

"I think we should pull back though, just be friends for now. Like roommates."

"*Like roommates?*" he asked in disbelief.

"I just feel so confused. I miss you, I love you. I just don't know if it's right to be together."

"If it's right to be together?" He knew he sounded like a moron repeating her words, but he couldn't come up with a better response.

"Can you understand?"

"No. I cannot understand. I've been doing what you asked for, giving you space, but this is bullshit. I didn't do anything; I didn't even get to choose my parents. Nothing is different from before we knew, not really. Don't you see that?"

"It feels different," she said in a quiet voice.

Jacob got up from his chair and knelt beside her, so he could look in her eyes. He took her hands. "I want to be the kind of friends who get married and spend the rest of their lives together." She didn't reply, and he sat down on the floor and put his head in her lap. She stroked his hair, he relished her touch. "I'm not anything like my father; you have to believe me."

But he could tell by her silence that she didn't know what to believe.

JOYCE

THAT IS NOT going to happen again," she said, buttoning her shirt. "It was a mistake."

"Which part? I'm perfectly willing to be on top next time." Dan zipped up his pants and stopped to glance at his watch. "Shit, I'm going to be late."

"Really, there is no next time." They faced each other.

"I know. I actually want Laura back; this was a mistake for me too. It never happened, okay?"

"It never happened," Joyce agreed. "I'm not going to be the home wrecker this time around."

Dan pulled his shirt over his head and looked at Joyce. "You know, Laura didn't know about you for a long time. I think she would object to being called a home wrecker."

"Oh, would she now? So sorry."

"I don't blame you for feeling hurt by how things ended with us. But be angry with me, not her. She really was young and innocent."

"Me too, Dan."

"Yes, you too." He put his arms around her. "You will always be my first love." She untangled herself from him and held out her hand. They shook hands formally.

"Goodbye, Dan."

"Goodbye, Joy. Joyce."

As he walked out the door, she couldn't help but to feel that he chose Laura all over again.

When Dan called her yesterday at the restaurant and wanted to meet, she had no intention of touching him, much less sleeping with him. He said he would make the drive to Tulsa, but she didn't want to meet at work—too many eyes would be on them, too many potential questions. She suggested he come to the house where they could talk privately; figure out how to make this easier on their kids. But they never even got to discussing Jacob or Cassie. She didn't even recognize her behavior, not that he needed much prodding. She wanted to be in charge, to be in control; she seduced him, if she could admit the truth.

Her sexuality had been bottled up for so long that when it got even this smallest of an opening, it just took over. No expressions at all of it since Andy died; not even touching herself. She couldn't bring herself to, not with what happened to him. She went from regularly making love with her husband, even shaking things up with tools or videos or location (*Let's do it in the office,* she once said to Andy during an especially long day at work), to shutting the spigot to the OFF position overnight. When she was with Dan for those moments she felt so good, so alive. But after it was over, she felt hollow, as if the only thing she accomplished was proving to herself that she could have him again. The thought of Laura finding out horrified her—she wanted to make the situation better for Cassie, not more complicated. She didn't need to pay Amy a hundred and fifty dollars an hour to see that part of being with Dan was some juvenile attempt to get back at Laura. *Pathetic*, she thought as she brushed her hair and touched up her makeup.

Equally pathetic was still going to see Amy to please her sister. A waste of time and money. Even with this new Dan wrinkle in the mix, Joyce felt stronger, better able to deal with what was thrown at her. Maybe Amy helped, maybe the marathon training helped, maybe it was just time. She decided to break up with Amy via e-mail the next day.

Maybe her sketch helped, she thought as she pulled it from a desk drawer. She had taken it home after a shift manager was holding it up in the air one day, asking her what it was, as he was getting change from the safe. She had returned it after her last revisions to the wrong safe, the one that managers had access to. She snatched it from his hand and took it home. Here she felt free to work on it openly, without having to listen for footsteps outside her office. She could actually look at the closet and not just envision it in her mind's eye.

She had made a lot of progress on it. The bed with all of her blouses, stacked with their hangers, was finished. The closet door, with its four recessed panels and shiny doorknob was completed. She had paid a lot of attention to the surrounding details inside the closet: the texture of the carpet, the clothes left on the high rod like dresses and winter coats, the framed picture of her on the floor in her swimming suit from years ago, the simple kitchen timer that was on the carpet, its hand pointing to the zero. She thought she should start with Andy now, place him in this scene that she had carefully put together from her memory. But this was the hard part, the very hardest part, and she had to take a few deep breaths before getting started.

She began with his shoulders and back as she first saw them from the doorway, trying to get the angle just right, showing their strength but as they were hunched over. Tapering the angle from his shoulder blades to his waist, she was surprised by a knock on her front door. She placed her sketch back in the drawer as she went to answer it. Did Dan come back?

But it was Pedro behind the screen door, showing off his dimples. "Hello, Joyce. I'm sorry to intrude on you at your home. Can I talk to you for a moment?"

"Yes, of course, come in." She led him inside to the living room. The door to her bedroom was still open, the bed a mess; thank God he hadn't arrived thirty minutes ago. She sat in an easy chair, he on the couch. She had only seen him once before not in his cooking uniform, in "civilian" clothes, the night that he drove her and Maggie home after their night of drinking at the Mexican restaurant. He had on a simple black T-shirt and jeans and looked freshly showered.

"What's going on?" she asked, all of a sudden worried that something may have happened to Maggie. "Is everything alright?"

"Yes, everything is better than alright, everything is great. I came here because I wanted some privacy to ask you a question. I hope you aren't upset that I came; I remembered the address from the night I brought you home."

"Sure, I'm available, no problem. What is it?"

"As you know, Margaret and I are going to have a baby. . ."

"Yes, it's wonderful news. Congratulations, I am so excited I get to be an aunt."

"You may have been wondering what our plans are?"

She hadn't really, other than raising the baby, of course. "Well?"

"I want to ask her to marry me. It may seem old fashioned, but I came to get your blessing to propose to her."

"You want my blessing? To propose?"

"Family is important to me, Joyce. I still have dinner with my parents and siblings every Sunday. You and Cassie are Margaret's family. If she marries me, we will all be one. Yes, I'd like your blessing."

Joyce was without words. Pedro jumped back in and pulled a piece of paper from his pocket. "Take a look at this and tell me what you think. I designed it for our wedding rings." She looked at the small drawings, simple bands with a heart. "They are tattoos for our ring fingers. I thought that would be better than rings."

"Yes, that is better than rings." She handed the paper back to Pedro. "You have my blessing to ask her. She would be a fool not to marry you."

He stepped forward to hug her then leaned back to look at her face. "Why are you crying?"

She hadn't realized she was. "Joy, Pedro. I am crying with joy."

CASSIE

SHE AND JACOB were taking a study break by looking online at state parks and nature trails in San Diego. They were researching areas to sprinkle her daddy's ashes, wanting it to be both stunningly beautiful as well as something dramatic. They weren't talking about a wedding in San Diego like they had been, but being in the same room with him gave her such peace and relief. They were sharing the same bed but had so far been treating one another like tentative teenagers—holding hands, spooning, gentle kisses.

"This one looks interesting," he said, pointing to his laptop. "El Cajon Mountain. Stunning scenery but looks like a hard hike. How difficult of a hike do you want if you guys are also running a marathon?"

"Good point, probably not anything too tough." She pointed to her own laptop, and then stopped herself. She was going to bring up the idea of taking his ashes to the beach, but thought better of it. They always talked about having the wedding on the beach.

"Will you come back with me for John's game? We

don't have to stay the night."

"When are you leaving?" The thought of seeing his parents made her heart thump loudly.

"I need to leave by four o'clock tomorrow if I'm going to make it on time."

"Oh, I thought the game was tonight." Her plan on him being out of the apartment for a while this evening was unraveling. She wouldn't have any time alone after all.

"You can think about it. It would mean a lot to me if you came. My parents love you, you know."

She knew that they loved her; she just wasn't sure how she felt about them anymore.

"Jacob, there's something I need to talk with you about." She didn't think she could wait until he left tomorrow. She needed to do it tonight.

"Okay." He looked so scared. He closed his computer and waited.

"Part of why I've been such a freak lately is that I'm late." She came over and sat next to him on the couch.

"Late for what?" he said earnestly.

She smiled. "You know, *late,* late."

His expression turned from fear to surprise. "Really? You're still on the pill?"

"Yes, but I'm still late. Nothing's a hundred percent guaranteed, except for abstinence of course." She smiled again.

"Oh, wow, I don't know what to say. Is it wrong to feel excited?"

She just shrugged, not knowing how to answer either. She went to her purse and pulled out a small rectangular box. "I got a pregnancy test. I was going to take it when you went to the game, but I think we should do it together."

They sat down and read the instructions together, including all of the fine print. Both in their tiny bathroom, he handed her the stick with the absorbent end to pee on. He counted to five as she held it in between her legs. They placed the cap back on and put it on the counter. She set the timer on her phone for five minutes.

"Come on," she said, grabbing his hand, "let's not wait in here."

She went into the kitchen and grabbed a pint of Ben & Jerry's from the freezer. She took a bite from Cherry Garcia. "My mom will shit if I get pregnant in law school."

Jacob got a spoon and took a bite from the container. "She'd get over it. Besides, Hillary Clinton had a baby in law school and look at her career."

Cassie frowned. "I don't think she was in law school when they had Chelsea, actually."

He shrugged. "Maybe not, but it sounded good, didn't it?"

Laughing, she put down her ice cream and punched him playfully on the shoulder. He caught her arm and pulled her to him. "I love you, Jacob," she said before kissing him. It started slow and steady but quickly unfurled into groping hands. She reached for the bottom of his shirt to take it off when the timer went off. Breathing heavily, they went hand-in-hand down the hallway to the bathroom.

"You look first," he said.

She looked at the test, not wanting to disturb it. She looked back at the printed instructions, then again at the test. She had tears in her eyes.

"What? Tell me, what does it say?"

"Not pregnant. Only one line in the box. I'm not pregnant." Tears were now freely falling. "I don't know why I'm so upset." Though she suspected, but didn't want to say; she would get to marry him if she was pregnant.

"I know why," he said, holding her in their tiny little bathroom. "You're upset because you want to have a baby with me. I do too, Cassie. I do too."

She had wished that the decision would be taken from her; to be forced with the news of a pregnancy into the marriage she wanted but felt so conflicted about. But she was beginning to understand that sometimes wishes just don't come true.

DAN

HE RECEIVED A text from Jacob that said: Cassie and I will be at the game today. Don't fuck this up for me.

Okay. What else could he say?

He wondered what Jacob's version of fucking it up would be. Having sex with Cassie's mom, certainly. It was the wrong thing to do, but he felt utterly defenseless in the situation. He just wished it hadn't been so *good*. Joy had been like a woman possessed; the combination of her aggressiveness and the vague sense of familiarity were intoxicating. He vowed not to be in the same room with her alone again. And though he knew it was wrong, it somehow seemed less wrong than being with Amber or another student because they used to be married. Nevertheless, on Monday he would talk to Phil about strategies to avoid a repeat scenario.

Preparing for the game in his hotel bathroom, he shaved and put on a light splash of aftershave that was Laura's favorite. He even flossed his teeth; he wanted to look good for her. He tried to redirect his thoughts from the afternoon at Joy's house to the last time he was with Laura in the kitchen. *Focus on Laura,* he told himself.

And when he saw her with the boys on the field before the game started, it was easy to. She was laughing with them and giving high fives, totally relaxed, comfortable, and beautiful. He stood back and watched, soaking it in, hoping she would come over to him. She finally did when the game started.

"Jacob and Cassie are supposed to show up," she told him.

"Yes, he texted me. He told me not to fuck it up for him. How am I doing so far?"

"So far, so good. But here they come," she answered, nodding to the far side of the field. They walked holding hands, Cassie with Jacob's ball cap pulled low so that you could barely see her eyes.

"She doesn't look like her mom at all, does she?" Laura asked.

"No, not really."

"She looks more like our family. Look at them, they could be siblings."

It was true; they had the same sunshine-tinged coloring. "Come on, Laura."

"There's nothing else I need to know about is there?" she asked. "Children left behind with Joy?"

Now that pissed him off. "Jesus, you think I could abandon a child?"

"No, I'm sorry. This has been hard, brought up a bunch of old garbage, you know?"

"I do. But you know everything about what happened with Joy already, you have for a long time." Well, *almost* everything.

"Here they come, I'll try not to fuck it up either. Let's talk after the game," Laura said.

And he had hope once again—they had a date after the game.

Jacob and Cassie walked up to them and Laura gave them both a hug. Maybe Dan imagined it, but Cassie seemed to stiffen in Laura's arms. He smiled and waved, feeling glad that he was standing at Laura's side when they showed up.

"Hey guys, glad you could make it," Dan said. "Just got started, nothing much happening yet."

"We'd like to take the boys for ice cream after, but then we need to split," Jacob said.

"Sure, that would be great," Laura said, for once not trying to get Jacob to stay longer. Dan was hoping it would give him an opportunity to be alone with his wife for a few minutes.

And it did, after an hour and a half of standing in near silence with Jacob and Cassie, and losing horribly to the opponent, he was left standing with Laura when the rest of them loaded into Jacob's car.

"Join me for a drink? At the Lodge?" There was no chance of seeing any of his students at the Lodge.

"Okay, sure," she said.

They drove separate cars there, giving it the feel of an illicit rendezvous. He felt himself become aroused, but tried to push away all of that. Following behind her in to the bar, he found it increasingly difficult.

"Scotch?" he asked, sitting down at a small cocktail table.

"Okay." She smiled. "I haven't had one in a long time." He suspected she hadn't had one since he left, that it would have reminded her of him. More hope ballooned his spirits that she would have one now with him.

"Dan, I've been thinking about something. . ." He was holding his breath, waiting for her to finish her sentence.

"Okay, tell me," he finally said.

"I want to go back to graduate school, get my masters or maybe even a PhD." She stopped and waited. He got the sense that his reaction to this news was important, some kind of test.

"That's a great idea, honey, I think you should."

"Really? Are you just saying that? To be nice?"

"No, I'm saying it because you're smart and it's a good idea to do something for yourself. But I am hoping it will make me irresistible," he added.

"It's just been so long since I've been in a classroom, except for one of the boys'. The thought makes me nervous."

"You'll be great, really. But you know how academia is, full of blowhards. Just be careful or you might turn into one. Like me."

"You're not a blowhard, Dan." She sipped her scotch.

"I'll support you if you want to do it. Or if you don't, either way."

"Thanks, that means a lot." They sat sipping their drinks, Laura tearing the corner of her paper cocktail napkin.

"Laura, something needs to change. We can't keep going on like this." She didn't respond. "The hotel is making me crazy. I've found a small house that is a good value. I should make an offer if I want it. But I don't want it, I want to come home. I want our family back. Please give me another chance."

She looked him straight in the eye. "I want our family back too. I'm just not sure if I want you back."

"I deserve that, but let me try, let me prove myself to you." She appeared to be thinking about it, definitely a good sign.

She drained her drink. "Okay, you can come home. But I want you to continue to see the therapist, okay? I don't want to be pressured to go unless I want to."

"Yes, yes, yes," he said with a wide grin.

"And I want you to stay in the guest room."

"Whatever you say, no problem." It was only a matter of time before everything fell back in to place. Finally.

MAGGIE

MAGGIE WAS SLEEPING, sprawled out on her futon when Pedro nudged her.

"Your phone," he said. "It keeps ringing from the kitchen."

She hadn't heard anything; her fatigue was overwhelming. "It's probably Tommy, having trouble with the alarm system. He's never opened before. Shit, I'm so tired. . ."

Pedro rose and brought her phone to her. It wasn't Tommy, it was an unfamiliar number and it had left two messages. After hearing the first sentence of the message, she sprang out of bed to throw on some clothes.

"Will you cover for me at work for a while?" she asked Pedro, who was now making coffee.

"Sure, what's going on?"

"I'm not sure yet. Joyce is in the hospital, I need to go see."

"The hospital? Let me go with you."

"I'll call when I find out what happened. I could really use you at work, especially with both me and Joyce not there." She found herself going into flight-attendant mode, very calm. Once when a man toward the front of the plane had a heart attack and died aboard, she had to reassure the rest of the plane that everything was fine, just an ill passenger. The event gave her practice on distancing herself from difficult events.

"Of course, I'll go in now. I will say a prayer for Joyce." He held her face in his hands and kissed her.

The hospital was close, only five minutes away. She pulled into the parking lot and saw that Cassie's car was already there. In an area of the ER partitioned with cloth walls, she found Joyce lying in a bed with an IV, her eyes closed. Cassie sat next to her in a chair, texting with an urgency on her phone.

"What the hell happened?" she whispered to Cassie.

"I can hear you. I'm not asleep, just resting," Joyce said from her bed.

"Okay, then," Maggie raised her voice, "what the hell happened?!"

"Mom was hit by a car. While running this morning," Cassie answered, putting her phone down.

"Oh my God, are you okay?" Maggie asked.

"I'm going to be fine," she answered, barely able to keep her eyes open.

"She will probably need surgery. We're waiting on the x-rays to come back, but her wrist got smashed."

"Hit by a car? What happened?" Maggie asked.

"Too tired now, damn medicine," Joyce said, dozing off.

Cassie motioned for Maggie to leave the area and they walked to the waiting room.

"The car that hit her actually brought her in," Cassie told her. "She was running downtown really early, it was still dark, and a car was coming out of the alley on Eighth Street. She had her headphones on, obviously didn't hear the car. The car didn't see her either." She started crying into her hands.

Maggie put an arm around her. "She's going to be fine, honey. Don't worry, she's a tough chick, just got a little banged up."

"It feels like my fault. She wouldn't have been running if it weren't for me. She could have been killed!"

"There, there, don't be so dramatic. She was running because she wanted to, she's an adult. Don't take this on."

"Don't take this on? Really?" she asked. "How can I not take this on? She doesn't have anyone else now, I *have* to take this on. You should have seen her when I first got here, so small, so vulnerable. She's alone, I need to be there for her."

"Cassie, you are there for her, what are you talking about? You were the first one to get here, your mom knows how much you care."

"I can't marry Jacob, I don't know what I was thinking."

"Now you aren't making sense. One has nothing to do with the other. You must be in shock or something. Let's go to the cafeteria and get some coffee."

"Maggie, I don't know what to do anymore. Help me," she said, putting her head on Maggie's shoulder.

"I'll try," Maggie said, having no idea how "I'll try."

LAURA

SHE HADN'T FELT so happy since she and Dan were first married. He was trying so hard—doing the laundry, picking up the boys, cooking dinner—she knew it wouldn't last but didn't care. The time away from him made her appreciate his good qualities even more: the dumb jokes he told at the dinner table, his compliments on her appearance, the way he patiently listened to her babbling on. The boys were glad to have him home; she even admitted to him that she was too. It was almost as if the Joy dinner had never happened.

Until she heard from Jacob, hysterical on the phone, saying Joyce had been hit by a car.

"Maybe one of us should go there?" Laura said to Dan. "To be with Jacob. He sounded really upset."

Dan looked at her in a peculiar way. She couldn't quite read his expression.

"Why don't you go," he said. "Jacob is still angry with me, I don't want to make it worse. Plus, maybe you'll get some time with Cassie. I think that might be good for her."

Laura honestly had not thought much about Cassie since the dinner; she had been focused on Joy, Dan, and her own role in the fiasco. Maybe Dan was right. This poor girl had been through the ringer. This was the girl her son planned to marry.

"I'll take care of picking up the boys today, I just have a morning class to teach," Dan said, ever accommodating.

Driving to Tulsa, she realized how rarely she drove any significant distance alone anymore. There was almost always a boy in the car with her, asking her to change the radio station, if she had a snack, or just taking off their shoes with their smelly feet. She wished she had a convertible instead of the gas-guzzler SUV, and for a moment felt that freedom she that remembered from the driving scenes from *Thelma & Louise*—head scarves flying, laughter, and sunglasses. Then she recalled that in the movie, the two women were actually running away, not truly free. Was she running away too?

She texted Jacob as she was gassing up on the highway: On my way to Tulsa. Can I meet you?

He texted back right away. On my way to class. Taking notes for Cassie. I'll text when I can.

Now she had an unexpected burst of time. What would she do? Maybe a movie, something romantic and sappy that Dan wouldn't want to see. Or shopping in some of the quaint downtown boutiques? Browsing in the university bookshop? But her initial energy was deflated, she was now just tired. She plugged in Jacob's address into her GPS and decided to wait for him at his apartment. After stopping for a caramel latte, she waited on a bench outside his apartment building. Looking for a napkin in her purse (how did she always manage to spill through the tiny hole in the lid?), she looked up to see Cassie in front of her.

"What are you doing here?" Cassie asked. Cassie's hair appeared un-brushed and it looked like she was wearing her pajamas.

"We were so worried about you all. How is your mom?"

"You're worried about my mom?" she asked, then muttered, "Yeah, right."

"Can I get you some breakfast or a coffee?" she asked, trying to ignore Cassie's apparent hostility toward her. "This latte is delicious. I'm blowing my morning's calories for it, but it's worth it."

"No, thank you. Does Jacob know you're here?"

"I texted him on the way and he said he was going to take notes in class. I was just waiting. Is there anything I can do?"

Cassie ran her fingers through her hair. "No, I just came

back to shower. My mom is in recovery now, she had surgery on her wrist."

"Oh, I'm glad it was nothing more serious. Getting hit by a car can be awful."

"It felt serious to me, actually."

"Of course it did, that's not what I meant. She'll be okay?"

"Yes. I guess so." Cassie looked at Laura with a strange mixture of pity and contempt. "Do you want to come in to wait? We have some banana bread I made yesterday."

"That sounds wonderful, thank you." Their apartment was much nicer than Laura had expected. When Jacob lived with two other male roommates, the place was a complete dump. This was tidy and clean, framed prints on the wall, magazines fanned out on the coffee table.

Cassie brought a plate with a few slices of the banana bread on it. "Do you need water or anything?"

"You don't have to wait on me. Thank you for your hospitality." Cassie turned to leave. "I always wanted a daughter. Every time I was pregnant, I was convinced it was my girl. Four times wrong."

Cassie gave her a stiff smile and, again, turned to leave.

"With Sam, I was convinced the sonogram was wrong even. I looked it up online, mistakes happen all the time. Her name was going to be Julia, keeping with J names like the others. And as happy as I was that he was born healthy, I was crushed Sam was a boy. We hadn't even chosen a boy J name. So we named him Samuel after my grandfather."

"I need to get in the shower. Sorry, I want to get back to the hospital."

"Your mom is lucky to have you. Not just because you are a girl of course, but because you are a special girl." Laura wanted to encourage her; Cassie seemed so drained and sad.

"You don't know anything about my mom," she replied, with a sharp edge in her voice.

"That's true. I never met her before last week."

"You did manage to meet her husband, however."

Laura knew that if she was going to try to help her son, she was going to have to have this conversation. She didn't want to, it still pained her to talk about it.

"Cassie, I don't expect you to understand. I was so young, years younger than you and Jacob. I didn't even realize what I was doing, the consequences my actions had."

"You didn't realize it was wrong to sleep with a married man?"

"I was young and stupid and didn't even know he was married at first."

"Oh, I see. So it's Dan who's the bad guy in this story?"

"There are no bad guys most of the time in real life. Just people, trying to do their best." She felt lighter just saying that out loud. Maybe she could forgive him. "Dan moved back in the house. I'm not sure if Jacob even knows yet. Dan is far from a perfect husband, to me or to your mom all those years ago. But we are going to try again."

"I guess he hasn't had a chance to meet someone else yet. How did it feel being the other woman?"

"It felt awful. But I had to keep moving forward, like I did then, like I am now. The same as your mom did."

"I wish she could now," Cassie confessed, softening. "Since my daddy died, she's been stuck."

"I can't imagine how hard it must be. But your happiness will help her; a mamma's heart is always with her kids."

"Well. . . I'm going to get in the shower." The sharp tension now dissolved.

"Okay, honey, thanks for the banana bread, it's delicious. I think I'll just write off this whole day of calories," she said, laughing. Cassie was walking down the hallway. "And remember, if your mom and Dan hadn't gotten divorced, there would be no Jacob. Or Cassie."

Cassie didn't respond, she just kept walking and closed the door behind her, leaving Laura with two more pieces of banana bread to finish off.

JOYCE

SHE HATED EVERYONE treating her like she was an invalid because of her wrist. Part of it was how foolish it was to let herself get hit by that car; she had forgotten to put on the reflective vest that she had purchased expressly for that purpose. And because of it, now her well-meaning family was cautioning her before she crossed the street like a five year old. When she returned to work a couple of days after the accident, Maggie asked her in surprise, "What are *you* doing here?"

"What do you mean? This is my restaurant, I'm at work of course." She held up her wrist, wrapped in a bandage. "No cast, even, just a few screws on the inside."

"Joyce, I was there when the doctor talked to Cassie. He said to take the week off."

"I'm fine. What's the deal? Now you want me to stay at home and isolate myself?" she snapped. "Make up your mind." Her wrist was actually throbbing, but she was tired of staying at home watching TV and surfing the Internet.

"I have an idea," Maggie said, putting her arm around Joyce's shoulders. "Why don't you go have an eat-pray-love-type adventure? Travel the world in search of clarity and enlightenment. . .take an Italian lover. . ."

"I'm the Julia Roberts character in this fantasy? Ha! If I didn't know better, I would think you are trying to get rid of me." But hearing the words "take a lover" made her think of Dan and shudder.

"Never. You just deserve a break."

"You're the one who's pregnant, I think you deserve the break. How have you been feeling?" she asked, glad to get the attention off of her.

"Fine, just tired. I understand that might improve in the second trimester."

"If I were you, I would get settled in with the idea of being tired. It doesn't end for a long time."

"Thanks a lot. Maybe you could lie to me a little?"

"I'm sure the second trimester will be much better," Joyce said with a grin.

"Pedro told me he got your permission, by the way," Maggie said, suddenly serious.

"He's a keeper, Maggie."

"I know. I can hardly believe how things have turned

out. And I want to thank you. If you hadn't given me the chance to run the kitchen, I would never have met him."

"It's funny how things can work out, isn't it?" Joyce said. "You've been great here, I don't know how I could have stayed open without you."

"Oh shit, I think I'm tearing up," Maggie said, wiping her eyes.

"That's why I want to talk to you and Pedro about becoming partners. In a modern Mexican concept. Here." When Joyce woke up from surgery and saw Maggie in a chair by her bed hunched over her laptop, making a food order, she knew it was what she wanted to do. What Andy would want her to do.

"Now I'm really going to start bawling," she said. "Let's go to your office, I hate the staff seeing me emotional."

"I think I'm going to leave after all, my wrist is killing me. Why don't the three of us talk about the details tomorrow?"

"You have no idea how much this means to me," she said before going back to the kitchen.

Joyce did want to go home, but it wasn't because of the pain. As she was looking into Maggie's face, full of surprise and joy about the offer, she thought of Andy's box of ashes in the storeroom. It felt like a punch in her gut that she had left him there. Suddenly ashamed, she went in search of it. Panicked when it wasn't under the linens she remembered, she found it pushed even further back in the corner. He was gradually getting buried among the forgotten and discarded items of the restaurant. She clutched the box and walked straight out the door.

At home, she put the box on her kitchen table and went for her sketch pad, determined to finish the sketch. Grateful her injury hurt her left hand so that she could still write, she popped one of the stronger pain pills she'd been given.

She finally finished the drawing satisfied that she captured it all. "Okay, Andy—there it is. That's how I found you." Maybe it was the medicine, but she realized then that she actually was one of those people who ended up talking to a box of ashes.

JOYCE

ANDY HADN'T RESPONDED to any of her texts or voicemails that she was coming home a day early. She didn't need a ride from the airport since she had left her car in the long-term lot, and wasn't surprised not to hear from him. He often didn't carry his phone when he was at work. But she did want to catch up and share some of the details of the wedding she attended without him in Florida, and to see how things had been for him at work.

One of the only friends she had kept from her college days had just remarried in Key Largo. Initially, Andy was going to go too. The trip was to serve as a much-overdue vacation. But their assistant manager walked out with no notice, the exhaust hood in the kitchen kept breaking down, and then (the final straw), a hearing with the state health inspectors about some bogus write-ups got scheduled during the time away. Joyce didn't think that she'd be able to get away at all, but Andy encouraged her to go anyway—*I'll take care of things,* he had said, *go have some fun, you deserve it.* The night before she left, they had stayed up late watching a re-run of *Jerry McGuire*, Andy dancing on the bed for her, shaking his bootie ("Show me the money!"), until she stripped him of his underwear.

And she did have fun. Fruity, rum-spiked blended drinks by the pool with her friend Denise, or just soaking up the rays and flipping through a magazine. The wedding itself was a surprisingly formal affair for a second marriage, but to each their own. Denise had meant a lot to her when she was so miserable in college; Joyce was happy to reconnect with her now in their more joyous days. Scheduled to be gone from Tulsa for four days, she could feel herself start to relax by the second. The resort offered sunrise yoga that she took advantage of, leaving her feeling calm and strong. It was a shame that Andy wasn't able to come, but she felt grateful that she had.

Because there was a tropical storm headed in their path and she feared complications getting home, Joyce changed her flight to leave out of Miami right after the ceremony, instead of the next day. It was a whirlwind getting to the flight on time and making her connection. She was excited and energized to get home.

But still no response from Andy as she buckled in to make the drive from the airport. She drove straight to the restaurant, thinking she would find him there behind the stove, with his phone sitting in the office as usual.

Theresa told her that he left after the lunch rush a couple of hours ago; she was expecting him back any time. Joyce left her luggage in the car and settled in the office to go through the tower of mail that had been ignored in her absence. An hour later, after filing everything, she glanced at her watch. It was past six o'clock and highly unusual for Andy not to be back. She looked in the kitchen, the storeroom, and the walk-in cooler. Thinking he met with Cassie for a run or a coffee, she sent her daughter a text. Andy's car was still not in the parking lot.

She drove home. Maybe he went for a bike ride during his break, got a flat tire, and was stranded on some country road. She was fighting her increasing irritation that she was getting worried over nothing. Many times she had been concerned about him on one of his adventures—skydiving or ski jumping—but he was always fine, and usually happy. *Don't be a ninny*, she told herself. *You've been through this before.*

Andy's car was in the driveway. Joyce parked next to it, grabbed her suitcase, and went to the front door. Locked. She scrambled for the key, having dropped her key ring back into the bottom of her purse. She turned it and stepped inside the entry. A setting sun sent diffused light through the open front door, revealing a light layer of dust on the surfaces. The house looked like she had left it days before—their brown leather sofa with the cable-knit throw blanket folded over the back, dining room chairs neatly arranged around the table, pink roses in a vase starting to brown around the edges of their delicate petals.

"Andy? I'm home early. Are you here?" she shouted.

No response. She was probably right, with his car in driveway he had likely gotten himself in a sticky situation on his mountain bike. She pulled her phone from her purse and pushed his name again on the screen to redial. She heard it ring from somewhere in the bedroom. She frowned, hung up, and walked to the back of the house. If he had forgotten his phone it could be a while before he would make it back.

She entered their bedroom and noticed a pile of her clothes on hangers laid out on their bed. Her first thought was that the house was being robbed; a neighbor told them that someone had broken into their car recently. But the front door was locked. There was no noise; she couldn't have interrupted an intruder, could she? The closet door, just off the bedroom, was usually kept closed, better to hide the clutter but now it was wide open. Her limbs felt a tidal rush of energy; fear surely, yet they moved forward, onward toward the door. She looked inside and the first thing she noticed was a timer on the floor, cheap white plastic, the kind that hardly lasted a day in the restaurant kitchen. It had a manual knob that turned to set it to the proper number. It pointed straight up to the zero. Next to the timer was an old photo in a simple black frame of herself in a bikini that she had forgotten about. Andy had taken it when they were in Mexico years ago; the sun caused her eyes to squint as she was doing her best to strike a seductive post toward the lens. Then she turned around wondering what these things were doing on the floor. . .

Andy was hanging by his neck from a brown belt on the lower rod of their closet. His legs were stretched out in front of him, his back to her, his naked backside hovering mere inches from the carpet. At first Joyce thought it was some sort of prank and let out a nervous laugh,

"That's not funny, Andy!" she said to no response. She touched his slumped shoulder; it was cool under her fingers. Her entire body felt as if it were being lightly pricked with needles, like when a foot falls asleep, but all over, even her scalp felt tingly. She seemed strangely detached until she stepped around to face him. Then she turned around and threw up on a pair of slippers.

Andy was holding his penis with both of his hands, semen trickled from the end and puddled on the carpet beneath him. A bright red bra of Joyce's was loosely hanging from his bent elbows. His dull gaze was directed toward the photo of Joyce in her swimsuit. But it was the lipstick, bright red and smeared on his open lips that flipped Joyce's switch to hysteria.

"Oh my God, Andy," she kept repeating, wailing with inhuman moans. All she could think to do was to get him down, but she couldn't figure out how to detach the belt from the rod; her hands wouldn't work, his body was so heavy. Finally she was able to lift the end of the rod without any clothes on it from its attachment to the wall, lowering the whole rod down on the floor. His head dropped, hitting the carpet with a heavy thump. He fell to his back, arms dropped stretched out to his sides. She had to get that belt off, must get the belt off, and when she wrestled it from his neck—it was so tight—and lay it open, a red line was left on his neck. She collapsed on top of his chest, heaving with sobs. When she looked up at his face, his beautiful face, all she could see was the lipstick. Suddenly possessed with an urgency to clean him up, she looked around the room. How could she clean him?

She squatted behind him and hooked her arms under his shoulders. Using all of her strength, she dragged him from the closet, the carpet made it so hard, it slowed her down, until she needed to rest. She was completely out of breath, sweat pouring from her temples, by the time that she got him in the shower. Propped up against the far wall of their open shower, she slumped next to him on the gray tile. She grabbed the nearest towel she could find and wiped what she could of the lipstick off and tossed the scarlet-smeared white cloth to the side.

Once she caught her breath, she did the only thing her racing brain could think of. She turned on the shower.

As the hot water steamed up the bathroom, she just stared at the water falling, striking her husband, and then disappearing down the drain. When she could hardly see anything because of the steam, she turned off the water and sat down next to him on the hot, wet tile. The water had pushed his hair over his face; she gently pulled it to the side. She remembered a time long ago when they had just begun to sleep together. They were in bed, exploring each other's bodies with their hands when Andy put his hands around her throat and asked, "Do you like it when I do this?" She had laughed and said, "I don't even like the pressure of a turtleneck sweater!" He removed his hands and they continued on. Why hadn't she asked him if he liked it? Why was he alone in that closet?

But she could still see some of the lipstick, and after trying to get the last bit off with another washcloth, she lightly kissed his unresponsive lips. "I'm so sorry," she told him through her tears.

She must have called 911, she didn't remember, but they showed up with sirens and an urgency to get in. Strangers poured into their house, she felt as if she were on a busy train platform in a foreign land and had no idea where she was going, which train to catch. A face came before her, "Is this where you found him?" it asked. She shook her head no and pointed to the closet. People were in her closet, looking at the floor, looking at the rod, looking at the belt. They nodded to each other, avoiding her eyes.

Suddenly she shouted, "Get the fuck out of my house!" They nodded to her and put Andy on a stretcher to take him away. *They are going to take him away,* she told herself, trying to stay connected to what was happening. *They are going to take him away, they are going to take him away, please don't take him away.* But they did, they started to take him away through the front door and she was left to wonder—*where will I go?*

JACOB

"WHAT IS WRONG with her?" Cassie asked, looking up from reading a text on her phone. "My mom wants to meet for a long run."

"Bull-headed, stubborn. Sounds like someone I know," Jacob teased.

"What is she trying to prove? I don't understand what this obsession is with her and the marathon now."

Jacob did. Wanting to woo Cassie had become his own obsession. He assumed that's what Joyce was doing too. "Seems better than hitting the bottle, I suppose," he replied. "Why not go?"

"She needs to rest. Her body has been through a major stress, Jacob."

"I don't know, she's a grown-up. Maybe indulge her with this?"

"Will you come?" she asked.

"How far are you going?"

"I don't know, she's saying fifteen, but I think she's

crazy."

"Do you want me to go?" he asked.

"Why do you think I asked you?"

He smiled and reached out for her waist. "Maybe you could say it, 'Jacob, I really want you to come with me. Please?' "

"Oh my God, you are so needy. Yes, I want you to come. Please!"

"Okay, I'll go. But I haven't run that far in over a year."

"Good thing you have youth and good looks on your side," she said, putting her hands behind his neck.

"Flattery will get you everywhere, but I already said yes." Although they were once again sharing a bed, the topic of the wedding had been off limits. He was hoping this run could be an opening. He recognized that it was risky, that it could backfire, but with Cassie's arms around him he felt reckless.

They met Joyce at the park not far from their apartment. Jacob thought she looked fine, but Cassie said, "Are you sure about this, Mom? You look really tired."

"Honestly, Cassie, I'm fine. Let's get started already. So glad to have you join us, Jacob."

They started out with an easy pace, chatting about the

weather.

"There's something I wanted to ask you both," Jacob said. "Just an idea to think about."

Cassie shot him a look, which he ignored.

"Sure, Jacob. What's going on?" Joyce answered.

Now that he started, he felt nervous. This had the potential to piss off Cassie, but he didn't see another way to get the wedding discussion back on the table. "Would you both be willing to have a dinner with my parents? I could cook this time, and have it at our apartment. I make a mean lasagna, really."

Cassie stopped on the sidewalk. "This isn't the time. What are you doing?"

"I'm sorry, but I don't know how else to move on. That meal was one of the worst experiences of my life. Not the food of course, Joyce, I didn't mean that, it's just that it might clear the air or something to try again."

Cassie definitely looked pissed, hands on her hips, jaw clenched. "I don't think it's. . ."

"I think it's a good idea," Joyce said. "Schedule it around what your parents can do."

"Mom," Cassie said, shooting Jacob another dirty look, "you don't have to do this. I'm sorry he blindsided you with it, I didn't know anything about it. Did I, Jacob?"

"She didn't. It was all my idea, I didn't even ask her about it. And believe me, I don't want to make things worse. I've got my own issues with my dad, you know."

Joyce cleared her throat, as if there was something she really wanted to say. "I'm actually glad to have this opportunity to say something to you two. Even though you're still in school and in my opinion too young, I think you should still get married. There's nothing that came out at that dinner that should prevent it from happening. You have my permission, you have my blessing."

Jacob rushed forward to hug Joyce, whispering "thank you" to her.

"And that is the second time this week I've given my blessing to a marriage. I must be getting old. Don't tell my feet that, though, I've been giving them a pep talk that they have abundant energy and ability," Joyce said.

"Maggie and Pedro?" Jacob asked.

Joyce nodded.

Jacob turned to his future wife, who stood silent with her arms to her sides, her face serious.

"Cassie. . . ?" he ventured. He hoped for a smile at

least.

"What about Daddy?" she asked Joyce. "How do you think he would feel about Dan in our lives?"

Joyce paused, appearing to think about the question. "You know what I think he would say? 'Water under the bridge.' That's what he would say. He'd probably thank Dan for freeing me up to be available for himself." She smiled at Cassie. "Doesn't that sound like him?"

Cassie nodded. "I could make tiramisu. We didn't get to eat it last time."

They did run fifteen miles after all, Joyce stopping to walk occasionally, Cassie at her side. But Jacob wasn't tired from the run like he thought he would be. In fact, he was exhilarated. Back at the apartment after the run, instead of reading criminal procedure, he devoted the next hour online, researching improvements he could make to his lasagna recipe.

DAN

HE HAD NO idea how good it would feel to sleep in his own bed again, to wake up and see Laura, head on her pillow like she was posing. The older boys initially gave him the silent treatment as he moved his things back in, and they grunted when Dan asked them to pick up their clothes from the laundry room floor. But soon things had returned to normal, reaching that comfortable rhythm that he had so missed.

Laura had returned from seeing Jacob and Cassie after Joyce's accident with an easy-going lightheartedness that was refreshing. Dan was determined not to screw things up again, to start with a clean slate. He was feeling confident until Laura told him about the dinner at Jacob's.

"They want us to come over on Sunday to their apartment," she told him when he returned from work on Friday. "Jacob's excited because he's planning on cooking."

"What's going on?" he asked.

"Joyce will be there. They want to have a do-over for

the last time."

"Joy will be there?" he asked.

"*Joyce*," she corrected him. "I don't know about the sister. I think we should leave the boys at home this time. I'll ask Rhonda if Sam can go over there until we get home. John and Jesse would let him eat potato chips for dinner."

He knew he would have to see Joy again, but didn't think it would be so soon. The image of her body, lean and sinewy on top of him, still felt fresh. He wished he could consult with Phil before this dinner, but he wouldn't see him until Monday.

"What do you think?" Laura was asking him.

"Sorry, what did you say?"

"I was asking if we should bring a bottle of wine or something for their apartment, or a plant maybe."

"I say wine. Maybe a bottle of scotch too."

"Is something wrong? I lost you for a moment there."

"No, no, just thinking about when I'm going to get some grading done that I've been putting off."

"Well, I think that this dinner is a good idea. You were right. It was good to have some time with Cassie last week when I drove over. She's a darling girl."

"Good. I hope this dinner is all Jacob wants it to be. Living in his displeasure is taking a toll on me."

Laura leaned next to him on the kitchen counter. "He'll get past this with you. I think he's just been so scared he would lose Cassie. But things are better between them now, he even feels optimistic about the wedding."

"I'm so glad, I hope he'll let me come."

"Maybe you could try to connect with Cassie? I think Jacob would feel better about you if she felt better about you. She could probably use a father figure in her life too."

"Yes, you're probably right." But as he thought about trying to win over Cassie, he imagined his clean slate as getting smeared. The kiss in his office. The romp in Joy's bed. A father figure to her daughter?

"Dad, you said you would play with me when you got home." Sam stood in front of him, tearing him away from his thoughts.

"Yes, of course. I've been looking forward to it all day. What's on the agenda?"

As Sam rattled on about his plans to construct a Lego castle that would rival all others, Dan renewed his resolve, telling himself not to fuck this up again.

MAGGIE

MAGGIE WAS NOT enjoying planning her wedding. Yes, she wanted to marry Pedro and start their family together. No, she didn't want to throw a bouquet, have birdseed thrown on her head, or any such dumb ritual bullshit.

"What do you want to do?" she asked him, hoping he would say go the courthouse.

"If we stay in Tulsa, we should do it at the neighborhood Catholic church. My family will want to be a part of it." His family was large and sprawling, all the more reason to elope, as far as she was concerned.

"Maybe we should wait until after the baby is born. Let her be a part of the ceremony from outside the belly," she offered.

"Her?" he asked, smiling. "You were saying 'him' yesterday?"

"I'm alternating days with gender references. If I'm supposed to have a mother's intuition on this then I suck."

"We should marry before she is born, Margaret. It's important."

"Let me think about it a bit longer. I promise, we'll have a plan soon."

He was so old-fashioned about certain things (being married before having a baby!). It was a quality that Maggie found exceedingly charming. Things were going so well between them that she found that she was waiting for the other shoe to drop. In the past, it always had. Which was why when she was looking through Pedro's backpack for a file with their new business projections and instead came across a bundle of envelopes from the U.S. Department of Homeland Security, her heart seized.

She texted her sister: Is there any way Pedro could be illegal?

Illegal? Joyce responded.

An illegal immigrant?

It took five minutes for Joyce to respond: Have all his documents on file. I don't think so. What's going on?

Talk later. Bye.

Maybe marrying her was just part of a plan he had hatched to become a U.S. citizen. Maybe he was never legal, she certainly never thought to ask. Was he using her? She should have known this was too good to be true.

Another text from Joyce: Why don't you just ask him?

Maggie didn't respond.

Maybe he didn't really love her. Maybe he would leave them once he got the marriage behind him. Maybe he would be dragged back to Mexico never to be seen again. Maybe, maybe, maybe—she could hardly think straight, yet couldn't bring herself to do the one thing that could bring clarity, talk to him about it. If the other shoe was to drop, let it be later.

"What do you think about California for the wedding?" she asked Pedro, as they were in the kitchen together later at work, trying to ignore the thump of her heart.

"California? I've never been there, sunsets and the beach, sounds wonderful. Where in California?"

"San Diego. I wanted to go for the marathon anyway. Maybe that weekend?"

"I thought Cassie and Jacob's wedding was then?"

"That was the plan, but we'll see. It's pretty touch and go with them right now."

He came over to rub her belly, just starting to pooch out. "You name the time and place, Margaret, I'll be there. Hey, maybe we could have one of those double weddings? I saw it in a movie once. Do they ever really happen?"

Maggie laughed. "Not that I've ever seen But I wouldn't want to take anything away from their day. Or from ours. But it could be a hoot. . ." *Pretend like you are fine,* she instructed herself, *beat back those voices for now.*

"I've never known you to be such a chicken-shit," Joyce said, catching her in the hallway to the restroom a few minutes later. "Come on, where's my sister? Beat your chest, get in his face and demand the truth."

"I know, it's just that. . ." She couldn't finish her sentence.

"You don't really want to know?" Joyce suggested.

"Something like that."

"I know exactly how you feel." Joyce took Maggie's hand and they walked back down the hallway, hand-in-hand, like they used to when Maggie was afraid to go into Sunday school by herself.

CASSIE

"I HOPE MAGGIE isn't miffed we're not having her and Pedro over too," Cassie said to Jacob as they were setting the table Sunday. "This place is just too small."

"We talked about it with her yesterday and I sensed no miffedness," Jacob said, taking some daisies out of a plastic sleeve and putting them in a vase for the table.

Ever since she agreed with Jacob that this dinner was a good idea, she was excited about it. They could show their parents on their own turf how compatible they were, how responsible and mature.

"So, what's the game plan anyway?" she asked.

"What do you mean?" he asked, placing the vase on the center of the table.

"I mean, what's the approach? 'Everything is fine. . . we're just a normal family thing?' Or 'let's talk about what happened last time so we can start over?' Or how about, 'let's tell the story of how everyone met.' I know, I know. 'When did. . . ' "

"Stop, please," Jacob interrupted. "I think I've got it.

How about we just let it unfold naturally? Go in with no game plan."

Cassie moved the vase of flowers from the center of the dinner table to the coffee table. "This is too tall to go there. It blocks your vision." She turned back to Jacob. "Sounds a little risky." She had grown weary of surprises.

"Is there anything you don't want me to talk about?" he asked. He was so sensitive; she couldn't believe she almost broke up with him.

"It's not us I'm worried about," she said, then added, "Although I don't feel the need to share I thought I was pregnant. Getting my period the next day, I felt like such an idiot."

"I look forward to telling them when you are pregnant for real." He pulled her in to kiss her as the doorbell rang.

Laura stood in the doorway, Dan slightly behind. Jacob hugged them, even his dad, then brought them inside. Cassie waved from the kitchen and tossed the chopped romaine with the Caesar dressing she had made. She intentionally stayed there to give the three of them a minute together alone.

"We brought wine and scotch," Dan said, handing them to Jacob. "What every household should have on hand."

He smiled, maybe a bit too large, too eager.

"Thanks, Dad, really. Should we open them both up?" Jacob seemed relaxed. "And I want to thank you both for coming, it means a lot to us."

Laura took the bottle of Sauvignon Blanc. "Yes, I'll have a glass. Do you have a corkscrew?" She looked closer at the bottle. "Oh never mind, it's a twist top. Jacob, wine? Dan, scotch?"

"No scotch, thanks. It's a long drive back. I'll just nurse a glass of wine," Dan answered.

"Let me help you, Mom. I'll dig out some glasses," Jacob offered.

Laura and Cassie exchanged light hugs in the kitchen and poured wine into glass jelly jars.

"Sorry we don't have any stemware yet," Cassie said.

"Maybe for a wedding gift?" Jacob suggested with a wink to his mom.

She laughed. "Let me take a look at your lasagna, mister." They huddled around the oven and Cassie grabbed a glass of wine to take to Dan in the next room. When she looked up, she saw Dan and her mom standing together in the front doorway. Their heads were leaning toward each other, too close, and Joyce's brow was deeply furrowed as she was listening to something Dan was saying. Joyce started to shake her head no when she caught Cassie's eye. The expression on her face immediately dropped then fell back into a smile.

"Hi, honey, I hope it's okay, I just let myself in. Dan and I were just catching up." Cassie realized that she hadn't even asked her mom if she had talked to Dan since the last dinner. It looked like they had.

"Of course it's okay, come in. Do you want a glass of wine? They brought a nice white." Cassie handed the filled glass to Dan.

"Take mine, Joy. . . Joyce. Sorry, it may take some time for me to get that right."

Her mom paused and then took the glass. "Thanks, but just one. I took a pain pill before I came. It's definitely better though." She held up her left wrist. "Dan, let me get another glass in the kitchen for you. I'll be right back." Cassie wondered if Joyce was intentionally leaving her alone with Dan.

"So, how is your semester going?" he asked. "Jacob says there's an unbelievable amount of reading required this year."

"Yes, it's brutal." Something was bothering her about the expression on her mom's face when she walked in. What did he say to her? Was it just the effect of her medication? "What were you two talking about when I came in? Sorry to be so nosy, but she had such a weird look on her face." She smiled, trying to keep it light.

"Oh, nothing. . . really . . ." he stammered. "You know. . . catching up, like she said."

Laura walked in the room, interrupting her next question to him, followed by Jacob and Joyce.

"Maybe we should get started?" Jacob asked. "Save the chit-chat for the table? I know you guys have to drive back and it is a school night for everyone."

They squeezed in on mismatched chairs around the small dining room table, a diner-style linoleum-topped number that was intended to seat four.

Jacob lifted his glass. "To family."

"To family," the others chimed in before clinking their jelly jars.

"Jacob, this looks delicious," Joyce said as they passed around the lasagna. "I'll tell you what I always tell Cassie. There's a job for you in the restaurant if the law thing doesn't work out."

"Although we'll have to learn to make tacos. . ." Cassie said and turned to explain to Jacob's parents. "My mom is partnering with her sister, Maggie, I guess you met her last time, and they're changing the restaurant concept. Modern Mexican, right, Mom? Do you have a name yet?"

"No, not yet. We're focusing on securing the financing for the remodel. None of the fun stuff like name or menu yet."

"Isn't that great?" Laura asked. "And good Mexican is so hard to find."

Cassie was feeling good about the conversation, all very light and safe. She let herself relax and drink the wine in front of her.

"My mom has a new plan too, don't you?" Jacob asked her.

Laura blushed, as if she didn't want to talk about it. "Well, I'm hoping to go back to graduate school next semester. Just trying to get all my ducks in a row."

"Jacob, you didn't tell me that," Cassie said. "That's great. We can all commiserate about our studies together. And complain about the professors too, of course."

She thought Dan might jump in, but he just smiled, as if he were distracted. A long pause followed as they chewed their food and Cassie wondered what she should say.

But Jacob broke the silence. "So, I just want to put it

out there since we're all at the same table. . ."

Shit, what's he going to say? worried Cassie.

"I appreciate, we appreciate," he said, gesturing to Cassie, "all of us being able to come together like this. We hope, now that we all know the truth, that we can go forward."

Everyone nodded, waiting for him to continue.

"Yes, about that," Dan said. "About the truth, that is . . . there's something I think I should say."

Cassie looked at the faces around the table: Jacob, head tilted, waiting; Laura, a smile frozen, lips stuck to her teeth; her mom, eyes wide as saucers, her jaw dropped, seemingly in horror.

"Dan, I'm sorry to interrupt," Cassie said, trying to think fast. "But I forgot to give an important message to my mom. From Maggie. It's on my phone in the kitchen. Can you join me in there?"

All heads swung to Cassie.

"What?" Jacob asked. "You didn't say anything about a message to me."

"Must have forgot, getting ready and all. Mom?" Joyce excused herself and squeezed out of her chair to join Cassie in the kitchen.

"Is something wrong with Maggie?" Joyce asked once they were there.

Cassie pulled her to the furthest corner toward the window and the potted plant. She lowered her voice. "What's going on with Dan?"

"What are you talking about?" she answered, looking flushed.

"Stop it. You know what I'm talking about." Silence. "Have you seen him since the last dinner?"

"Yes," Joyce answered with hesitation.

"And?"

"And, what? What do you want me to say Cassie?"

"What happened? You two are acting weird."

Joyce sighed. "Honey, these things are complicated. We have a history that goes way back—"

"We don't have much time." Then she asked the question that had been lurking below her thoughts since she saw them together. "Did you sleep with him?"

"Yes," Joyce said. "And I immediately regretted it, he did too. He wants to make his marriage work and I can assure you, I don't want to break it up."

"Oh my God. Wow, I didn't think that you would say

that. . ."

"I don't want to lie to you."

Jacob came in the kitchen. "Everything okay? I was getting worried."

Cassie turned to him. "Yep, everything's fine, no emergency after all. Come on, Mom, let's go eat."

They settled in back at the table.

"I hope you are all available to come to San Diego for the Wedding-Marathon-Extravaganza," Cassie said.

Jacob turned to her in surprise, his mouth in a wide-open smile. "Yes, the wedding-marathon extravaganza." He looked at Joyce. "You *have* to be there, because of the marathon, but what about you guys?" he asked his parents.

"Are you kidding, we wouldn't miss it," Laura said, looking at her smiling oldest son.

"And a fitting metaphor of marriage," Dan said. "I wanted to tell you all in person that I've moved back home. That I'm in love with your mother and we aren't giving up on our marriage." Laura reached for his hand.

Cassie again looked at the family gathered at her table. Jacob was beaming. Laura and Dan were gazing at each other. Her mom was looking down at her hands.

"How about this?" Jacob asked. "A *double* wedding-marathon extravaganza? We should totally get Mags and Pedro in on this."

Cassie laughed. "Yes. That would be perfect. Do both couples actually walk down the aisle at the same time?"

"Dan, we could renew our vows," Laura said. "It could be some sort of marriage party."

Dan looked at Joyce, who still stared down at her hands.

"Oh, Joyce, I'm sorry," Laura said. "That was really insensitive. Please forgive me."

Joyce looked up. "Don't be silly, this is a joyous occasion. Marriage is something to be celebrated, I couldn't be happier for everyone."

"May 31st is my daddy's birthday," Cassie said. "The day of the marathon. Mom and I are going to scatter his ashes there, aren't we?"

Joyce nodded and smiled. "The Double Wedding-Marathon-Ash-Scattering-Extravaganza?"

"Indeed," Cassie replied.

And this time they finished with tiramisu, and all agreed that Cassie's was better than any they had ever tasted.

MAGGIE

SHE *WAS* ACTUALLY a bit miffed that she wasn't invited to Family Dinner, Round Two, as she referred to it to Joyce. She imagined that she wasn't wanted there, that they didn't like Pedro (maybe Laura was racist or something), that she was getting pushed out of the family unit at the very point when she wanted in.

But Maggie knew she couldn't trust her emotions, spiraling away from her as they were, as if she occupied the body of a stranger. *Everyone hates me,* she thought when one person complained about their schedule at work. *I look like a whale,* when she was unable to button her jeans. *Pedro doesn't love me,* the thought that hurt the worst.

But Pedro acted like he loved her; nothing had changed in his behavior, certainly. If anything, he seemed more attentive and devoted. He massaged her feet at the end of the night, brought her maternity vitamins in bed, talked about names for the baby. She had never felt so confused.

Joyce sought her out in the kitchen on Monday, leaning in as Maggie was bringing the lineup for service, to privately share the details of what happened at Family Dinner, Round Two.

"Shut up!" Maggie said. "She asked you straight out, when they were in the other room?"

"I was so surprised and I actually told her the truth," Joyce said.

"The truth?"

"Oh, I didn't tell you. Last week Dan came by the house and, well. . ."

"Didn't I tell you to be careful? What in the hell are you doing?"

"I know, I am not proud of what happened. But you know what? It's been a long time for me. There was something that felt safe with Dan. It won't happen again."

"You never cease to amaze me. And you told Cassie?"

"She *asked*. And Dan wanted to come clean with everyone at the table, Laura included. Cassie diverted the whole thing. And now we have a wedding again. There was even talk of a double wedding. . ."

"Excuse me?"

"They brought it up. Don't you think it would be fun? And you could avoid the whole Catholic mass ceremony."

"Joyce, I need to talk to you."

"We are talking."

Maggie lowered her voice. "I just don't know what to believe about this immigration stuff."

Joyce leaned in closer. "You mean, you haven't asked him about it yet?"

She shook her head.

"I'll give you until tomorrow to bring it up with him. Or else I'll make up a story about getting a notice or something from the government and just ask him myself."

Maggie chewed on her thumbnail.

"Honestly, Maggie," Joyce said, "I don't know what you are so afraid of."

But instead of just asking him, as she knew she should, she waited until late that night, when she heard his breathing rise and fall into a deep pattern. She quietly slipped out of bed and went in search of his backpack, finding it next to the front door on a hook. She unzipped the top and reached around with her hands, trying to find the envelopes. They were at the very bottom, under a sweatshirt, a notepad, and a pack of gum.

The elastic that held the bundle together was taut. She removed it and started with the sheets inside the top envelope. How could people make sense of this bureaucratic bullshit? Much less people who don't speak English as their first language?

She sat down and tried to scan the information quickly. Finally, three pages in, she read that Pedro Perez had passed his oral and written exam. Future correspondence will be sent regarding the date for reciting the Naturalization Oath of Allegiance to the United States of America.

"What are you doing?" Pedro asked, standing in his boxers in the doorway. "I heard you leave and when you didn't come back right away I thought you were sick."

"Oh, Pedro, I'm such an idiot." The fear and insecurity that had been building up erupted into a flood of tears. She had never cried in front of Pedro, bawling with snot running down her face.

He came over to her and took the sheets out of her hand to read them. "I see. Let's sit down."

"You don't have to explain," she started. "I shouldn't have gone through your stuff. I don't know what's wrong with me. I've never felt so—I've never felt so afraid."

He held her face in his hands. "I didn't tell you what was going on. My mom would call that a lie. I'm sorry. It's just that I wanted to surprise you. I've been trying to become a citizen for almost five years now. I'm finally close."

"You are amazing, really. I am an asshole."

"What did you think I was up to anyway?" he asked, tracing the outlines of her bicep tattoo with his finger.

"No. I will not say it out loud."

"Margaret, I've always been legal. Soon I'll be a naturalized citizen. Our son will be born to two Americans," he said, grinning.

"So it's son, now?"

He shrugged. "It's Monday, isn't it? I thought we were alternating days with gender?"

"If it's a boy I've been leaning toward Jose, for your father," she said, scratching Pedro's back lightly the way he liked it.

"I've been thinking, between all my cousins there must be four or five little Joses running around. What was Andy's given name?"

"Andrew."

"Maybe Andrew Perez sounds good?"

She leaned over and put her head in his lap. "Andrew Perez. Maybe it does."

LAURA

SHE DIDN'T TELL Dan where she was going when she asked if he could pick up the boys after school, and he didn't ask. Nor did she tell him that she was taking the joint they had found in Jesse's underwear drawer the day before. When she got on the highway late that morning, she had actually told herself that she was going to surprise Jacob and Cassie, maybe take them to lunch to talk about the wedding. Even though she didn't want to be one-of-those-kind of mothers of the groom she did want to talk about it. The flowers, the dresses, the music, the fun details for her to think about. She just didn't want to seem pushy with her opinions or feedback. Jacob would hate that.

But she never texted or called him that she was coming, and when she got off the interstate in Tulsa, she found herself in the parking lot of Andy's Café. She supposed that it was Joyce she actually wanted to see. But when she asked the hostess if she was there, she was told that she hadn't come in yet.

"Can I talk to her sister? Maggie, right?" The teenage girl clearly looked uncomfortable with the request. "Let me get my manager." Laura just smiled, waiting with her purse clutched in front of her.

A few minutes later Maggie walked up to the hostess station. Her hair was pulled back in a ponytail, she had dark circles under her eyes, her chef's jacket was being stretched to its max at her belly. Laura felt a small pang of jealousy; she had an unexplainable desire to be pregnant. Even when she knew better, she couldn't help it.

Maggie stood in front of her with her tattoo-filled arms crossed in front of her chest, eyebrows raised in a question. "Yes?"

"I'd like to see Joyce."

"She's not here," Maggie said, not moving from her stance.

"Could I have her address? I'd really like to talk to her." She smiled. Maggie was really pretty actually, she could see a bit of Cassie in the eyes.

"You want to go to her house?" Maggie asked.

"Yes," she said, then paused. "Our kids are getting married, we are going to have speak to each other, don't you think?"

"Let me text her, she may be on her way already." She pulled her phone out of her chest pocket and with lightning speed shot off a text. They waited in silence until they heard the ding of a received message.

"Okay, she said to come over." Maggie looked up at Laura. "What's your number? I'll text you her address."

With no plan as to what she would say to Joyce face-to-face, she entered the address into her GPS and drove away.

JOYCE

SHE HAD JUST gotten out of the shower after her run when she got Maggie's text: Code red. Laura is here and wants to see you. Wants to come to your house???

Without thinking much about it, she responded: Send her over. To which Maggie replied: FYI She's wearing another cardigan. And then: Call if you need backup. And then: If you don't respond to my texts I'll have to assume that she shot you in a fit of jealous rage. I forgot to check her purse for a gun.

Joyce slipped into her work outfit, a simple blue dress, and typed to Maggie: It's all fine. I'll be in later. By the time she put on some lip gloss and mascara, she heard her doorbell ring.

Joyce knew sooner or later she would have deal with Laura. She actually preferred sooner, putting off the truth for later proved to be exhausting. She wasn't stressed at the thought of having Laura in her house, she was actually curious. What did Laura want from her?

She opened the door and saw Laura's face, set in a nervous smile. So pretty really, even with the extra weight she was the kind of beauty people did a double take for.

"Hi, come in. Maggie said you wanted to see me." She opened the door wide for Laura to enter. They stood in the entry, Laura clutching her purse.

"You have a lovely house, this is such a charming neighborhood," Laura said.

"Thank you. Andy and I bought it when Cassie was four, I can't believe it's been so long. Would you like something to drink? I don't keep much here, but I've got coffee or water. . ."

"No thank you, I had a latte on the way over. I don't know why I'm here. . . I'm sorry."

"Want to sit down?" Joyce asked, and they sat side by side on the leather couch in the living room.

"Dan told me what happened. Between you two here," Laura blurted out.

"Okay. . ." What was the correct response, she wondered?

"And the crazy part was that I wasn't even mad. Isn't that weird?" Laura asked. "It was the first time he had confessed anything to me. After years of hiding everything, it felt like a victory. Am I losing my mind or what?"

"I don't think so. I think I might understand."

"I understood why he would want you. I mean, look at you—*I* want you, you're so strong and successful, and of course, thin." Laura smiled. "You must think I'm a fool babbling on like this to you."

"I don't. And for what it's worth, I'm certain both of us regret the actions of that day. And honestly, I think I'm more at fault than he is."

Laura just looked at her. "I found a joint in my son's room yesterday. I was so surprised, Jesse is generally such a rule-keeper."

"I don't think it's as big of a deal anymore. I bet even Oklahoma will legalize it eventually," Joyce said. This conversation was feeling surreal. Was she really sitting at her couch having a conversation with Laura about marijuana?

"This morning I thought to myself that I'd like to try it. I never have." She grabbed her purse and pulled out her son's joint. "Do you want to smoke it with me?"

Joyce laughed. "You want to smoke your first joint with me?" It seemed to be the funniest thing she had ever heard, and they hadn't even lit up.

"Yes. I'd like to smoke my first joint with you. How's that for breaking the ice?" Laura joined in her laughter.

"Okay then, let's do it," Joyce said, even though she didn't really like being high. On her first day back at work after Andy's funeral, one of the kitchen guys slipped her a joint, help you relax, he had said. But it just made her want to sleep and she needed help getting out of bed, not in.

"Do you know how to inhale?" she asked, feeling like she had when she was in the basement with Maggie in high school and they wanted to try cigarettes.

"Yes, I've smoked cigarettes."

"This isn't the same. Just take a small one, okay? Stuff these days can be really potent."

Joyce found some matches in a kitchen drawer and took the first drag. It burned her lungs and felt really strong. She passed it to Laura, who while taking her drag, left her fuchsia lipstick on the joint.

"I don't feel anything, do you?" Laura asked.

"Not really." They both took another drag.

"When I suspected Dan was with someone else, he always denied it," Joyce said, feeling loose. "Told me I was being neurotic."

"I'm so sorry, Joyce, I really didn't know at first." Laura's eyelids started to drop slightly.

"And when I found out it was you," Joyce continued, "I followed you. For almost a week I practically stalked you. Going to your classes, to tennis practice, with your sorority sisters."

"I never noticed you."

"No. Dan didn't either. I knew I had lost him, I just felt so desperate. And when I saw you, I knew I didn't stand a chance. Not against you." Her lids were dropping too, she could feel everything begin to uncoil.

"That was back when I idolized Dan. Seems like a long, long time ago now."

"I thought I had put it all behind me, even after I saw you both at the restaurant. But I wanted to hurt you, I realize that now. I'm sorry I slept with Dan."

Laura nodded. "I think I'm stoned now. But nothing feels funny yet. I thought I was supposed to be laughing . . ." That was enough to crack them both up, laughing until tears fell down their cheeks.

"Whoa, the room feels like it's spinning," Laura said, stretching out to lay down on the couch. Joyce moved to the floor.

"Jacob is awesome," Joyce said and grabbed a throw pillow from the couch to put under her head on the floor. "Really. I think they are perfect together. If there is such a thing."

"No, it's Cassie who's awesome. I have never seen Jacob so happy," Laura said. "Am I slurring?"

"A little, but I can understand you."

"I hope they have kids soon. Maybe I shouldn't say that, but I do," Laura said.

"Andy was always looking forward to grandkids. Thought he might be able to create a little chef. Cassie was never interested."

Laura sat up. "I'm sorry about Andy. I just don't understand how a healthy person can just fall over dead like that. . . Should we finish it?" She held the remaining half of the stubbed-out joint.

"Sure," Joyce answered, certain she would not make it in to work anytime soon. "I better text Maggie. She'll worry. She thought you might have a gun." Her shoulders were heaving with laughter as she typed: I'll be late. Getting stoned with Laura.

"Now I'm getting hungry," Laura said. "This is not good for my diet. No more pot for me. How do you stay so thin anyway?"

"I don't eat much. Haven't been able to since Andy. . . Sorry, I doubt I have any food either. We could order a pizza? I don't think we should drive."

"No, no. If you don't eat, then I won't either. My

reaction to stress is the opposite, to eat more."

"Grief is different than stress though," Joyce said.

"I've never seen a dead body," Laura said, "Not even in a coffin. Not even a dead dog. Only in the movies. Doesn't that seem wrong?"

Joyce heard her but didn't answer; despite her inhibitions unraveling, her heart was beating so hard, so loud. She knew what she was going to do, what felt like she *had* to do.

"Can I show you something?" she asked. "Something I haven't shown anyone else in the whole world?"

Laura, her heavy lids concealing her beautiful blue eyes, nodded.

Joyce went for her sketchpad; her hands were trembling as she brought it back to the couch. She opened it, looking for the right pages, then she paused. "Have you ever heard of a gasper?"

"Like the ghost?" Laura asked.

"No, not the ghost. I hadn't either." Then she handed the open book to Laura. "This is how I found Andy. I had to draw it. I've never talked about it."

Laura looked down at the drawing lying down on her lap. Her eyes widened out of their laziness and her hand went to her mouth. She let out a small gasp. "Oh my God." Tears rolled down her cheeks, she kept her hand over her mouth.

Joyce didn't feel like crying, though. She, in fact, felt better. She took the book from Laura and closed it.

"I don't want that to be how you think of him. He was such a good man, so much fun, a loving dad. And he really did love me, and in a way Dan never did. I don't get to know what he liked about doing that," she nodded to the sketchbook, "but I do know those things about him. I do know those things."

So after they made microwave popcorn (the only food in the house they could find), they lay back on the couch and Joyce told stories. How she met Andy at that dumpy pizza joint. Their first kiss. The fight where she kicked him out of the car and made him walk home. When Andy carried Cassie home from school on his shoulders after the strap on her sandal had broken. Their plans to sell the restaurant and travel to Australia. She talked so long that when she looked over to Laura, she saw that she was sleeping. And feeling so very tired herself, she leaned her head back against the cushion and closed her eyes too, hoping that she would at least dream of her husband.

JACOB

JACOB LOOKED UP from the computer. "The ten-day forecast has wedding weekend dry and in the mid-seventies."

"Which is what it almost always is like in San Diego. Why don't we live there?" Cassie asked.

"We can live wherever we want, my beautiful bride," Jacob said, pulling Cassie toward him. "Are you sure you won't come with me to lunch?"

"I wasn't invited. I think your dad wants it to just be the two of you."

"But, I want you to. Pretty please."

"No, I'm going to the hospital anyway. Maggie said that Ann might get cleared to go home today."

"If that's true, then I want to be there." Jacob had visited Maggie and Pedro's daughter every day since she was born prematurely.

"Don't worry. She's got plenty of time to get to know Uncle Jacob. I've already been hit up for babysitting."

She laughed. "And it's good for you to have some time alone with your dad. If I can bond with your mother, then you can with your own dad."

He supposed she was right, but he still didn't want to go. His parents had entered into some new phase of being happy with each other, but he found going along with it to be an effort. To cut down on the driving time for both of them, they were meeting in the small town of Bristow at a diner.

His dad was there, sitting in a linoleum booth, when he arrived. He looked up from the menu and saw Jacob. He stood up and gave him a hug.

Jacob felt himself tense up in his dad's arms.

"I can't remember, what's good here? It's been ages. I think you might have still been in high school when we were here last."

"The chicken fried steak," Jacob answered. It *had* been high school when they were there last; Jacob asked to come before he went away to college.

Dan put down his menu. "Chicken fried steak it is. Good thing your mother's not here, she's been practically anorexic getting ready for your wedding."

"I wish she wouldn't obsess about her weight," Jacob said.

"I know. She is a beautiful woman. I wish she could see that more often," Dan said.

Jacob picked up a packet of saltines that were stuffed in a small bowl on the table. He wasn't particularly hungry, but it gave him something to do.

"So—ready for the big day?" Dan also opened a packet of crackers.

"Yes, I am more than ready," he answered, his mouth full.

"A little nervous? I know I was," his dad said.

"Which time?" he asked.

"Excuse me?"

"Which time were you nervous? With Joyce or with Mom?" Jacob asked.

"Both, actually," he answered.

The waitress stopped at their booth and took their order: two chicken fried steak platters with chocolate malts.

"Do you want to talk about it? About me and Joy?" his dad asked.

"It's Joyce, and no, not really," he answered.

"Cassie doesn't look like her, but now that I'm getting

to know her better, I can see a lot of her mother in her," his dad said. "So smart, but kind. And fun too."

Jacob just nodded and figured if he just let him talk, his dad would eventually get to why he wanted to meet.

The waitress delivered their malts.

"So, you may be wondering why I wanted to do this..." his dad began.

"A little," he admitted. "Why don't you let me guess...Mom's pregnant? No, she's too old. Your girlfriend is pregnant? No, you don't have those anymore, right? Let's see, there's another ex-wife I don't know about?"

"I can understand why you're angry with me, really I do." He stopped to drink some of his malt though a straw. "I've been seeing a therapist for a while now and it's really helped. I can't believe it, but it has."

"That's great, Dad, good for you," he said, not bothering to keep the sarcasm out of his voice.

"And I said something to Phil recently—that's his name—that he thought I should tell you directly."

"You don't have cancer or something do you?"

"Stop it. Let me talk please."

Jacob fell silent, feeling like he was ten years old again.

"I was telling Phil that I hope Jacob knows that he's going to be a better husband than I've been."

Jacob just looked at his dad.

"And Phil said, 'he'll know if you tell him.' So that's what I wanted to say, you aren't destined to repeat my mistakes. And I couldn't be more proud of you." He leaned over to drink more of his malt.

"Well, now you've said it," Jacob said, finally relaxing into the booth.

And then the chicken fried steak arrived, piled high on a mountain of mashed potatoes and green beans, and covered with rich brown gravy. Eating the food with his dad, Jacob couldn't believe how delicious it all tasted.

MAGGIE

MAGGIE PLACED ANN carefully in the yellow cotton sling that was worn over one shoulder and allowed her to use both hands while her child was cradled on her. Ann was so very tiny, but healthy and eating on her own. The sling served to keep her close, but because she was also tucked down beneath the folds of the fabric, it also kept germy hands away from her.

"Shit, why did I put her in the sling?" she asked Pedro. "I'm getting in the car, she needs to go in the car seat. My brain is not working. . ."

"Why don't you leave her with me?" Pedro suggested. "Have a drink, relax a bit. There's milk in the fridge and you can always pump when you get home, yes?"

"Not a chance, daddy-o. If I showed up without her I think I may get beat up." She stopped to kiss him. "But thanks for the offer. Will you help me get her strapped in the car?"

It was a short drive to Joyce's house for Cassie's bridal shower/bachelorette party. Cassie didn't really want to do it (too traditional!) but acquiesced under pressure from her mom and Laura. At first Maggie was perplexed by their strange new friendship, precipitated as it was by getting stoned together, something Joyce never properly explained to her after sending that crazy text. But she saw that Joyce was more relaxed these days, quicker to laugh, so who was she to judge?

Once she arrived, she got out of her car and put the sling back on. Every step of life took so much longer with a newborn; it took some getting used to. God forbid if she forgot her diaper bag, which happened frequently, and required her going back home to get it, starting the unload-load process all over again. She finally understood why new mothers complained about being unable to take a shower. It was all so exhausting. But to gaze upon their girl, little and fierce as she was, Maggie realized how lucky she really was.

She got Ann back in the sling, grabbed the diaper bag, the gift bag for Cassie, and put on her special headband for the occasion.

Joyce opened the door for her and burst out laughing.

"What? Is it not big enough?" She tried to look up at the penis protruding from the headband. She and Pedro had a blast shopping at what he called the "dirty store" for the accessory.

"Don't move! I want to get a picture." Joyce pulled her phone from her pocket. "Could you lift Ann up a bit?

I'd like to get her closer to the dick."

Laura came up from behind Joyce with her phone, too. "Smile! This is going on my Facebook for sure. Maggie, I'll get you a copy for Ann's baby book."

Cassie extracted herself from a group of her law school friends. "Could you keep it down? You're embarrassing me. I can't imagine how poor Ann feels. Gosh, Maggie, is that what happens to a newlywed, wearing phallic headgear?"

"Only if you're lucky," Maggie answered.

She and Pedro had married at the courthouse shortly after Ann's early arrival. He had smiled as they got their tattoos and said, "No more calling me baby daddy, yes?" to which she agreed.

Cassie laughed. Maggie lowered her head toward her, trying to get the angle just right for her penis to poke at her. Cassie opened her lips and pretended to take it in her mouth, rolling her eyes with apparent pleasure.

Laura dramatically put her hand over Joyce's eyes. "Please not in front of your mother."

And then without missing a beat, Joyce put her hand over Laura's eyes. "Or your mother-in-law!"

Maggie checked her phone and sent the text to Pedro's younger cousin: Now.

A moment later there was a knock at the door, where Miguel stood in a police officer's costume and mirrored sunglasses.

"Excuse me," he said with a smirk, "I've been notified of noise and. . . indecency complaints."

Maggie was pleased; he was totally sticking to the script. He lowered his glasses. "Is one of you the bride?"

Cassie held up her hand like she was in first grade and she really wanted to tell the teacher the answer.

"I'm afraid I'll need to question you." He pulled out a set of handcuffs and spun them on his finger.

The room roared with laughter.

Cassie held out her hands in front of her with a smile; Miguel clicked them shut around her wrists and led her to the easy chair. Maggie plugged her phone into Joyce's small speaker and pressed play on the song she had chosen for the dance. Everyone gathered around as he peeled off his uniform down to a speedo—even he was laughing as he held his arms above his head to dance. It was the best fifty bucks she had ever spent. It really was a shame that Ann slept through the whole thing.

CASSIE

SHE WAS A bit hung-over from the party. After the police officer dance, the champagne was opened and poured liberally. They played silly games like blindfolded pin-the-junk-on-the-hunk; a pecker toss; taking shots of something called Blow Job. She didn't know why she resisted the idea of a party, it was the most fun she had in ages. And who knows what Jacob's night had been like, he was still sleeping after being dropped off at the apartment after she went to sleep.

She crawled out of bed and went in search of Advil and a large glass of water.

She forgot to charge her phone before bed as she usually did, and it was almost dead. But there was enough juice to open a text from her mom. Look outside your front door. The sunlight that bore into her eyes when she opened the door was painful. She looked around and noticed a package at her feet.

A shoe-sized rectangular box, wrapped in Snoopy paper, the famous dog lying on top of his house, nose pointed in the air. She picked it up, it was light actually, didn't seem to be shoes. She carried it inside and saw

Jacob walking from their bedroom. He was running his hands through his hair, like something was stuck in it and then he stopped to smell his armpits.

"Remind me that tequila is not my friend lest I should ever forget. I think there was something involving Jell-O last night."

"Oh you think, do you? Anything I need to be worried about?" she teased.

He wagged his finger at her. "You have no room to talk, missy. You should have seen some of the pictures my mom sent me on my phone. My mom! If I didn't know better, I would think she was trying to break us up."

"Ha! Come over here and let me take a look at you." She put the box down and ran her fingers through his hair, feeling that it was sticky in places. She leaned over to smell his armpits; strangely a strawberry scent filled her nostrils. She took a lick. "Yep, I'd say Jell-O."

"Well, don't stop," he said. "I'm headed to the shower. Join me?"

"I want to open this box first," she said.

"Is it from the party?" he asked.

"I think Mom dropped it off today. I'll be in soon." She sat down and wondered what could be inside. Last night her mom had given her the commercial food processor that she had been lusting after as well as a beautiful silk nightgown. Just throwing the party had been enough really, she couldn't imagine what else she would get. She ripped open the paper and found the same shoebox that she had given to her mom, with the shoes inside, when she asked her to run the marathon. She lifted the lid and saw a piece of paper folded in half.

She opened it. "Some goodies to keep you going during the marathon. Thanks for keeping me going this past year. Love you, Mom."

Under the note was a photo she hadn't remembered seeing before: Joyce lying in a hospital bed, holding baby Cassie all bundled up like a potato, Andy leaning close to Joyce's face, holding a thumbs up with his left hand. Under the photo was a pair of high wicking running socks, a package of energy gummy bears, several Goos to squeeze in the mouth while running, and a sleek new running watch. Cassie squealed with delight.

She went to her phone to text her mom, but saw that she had received another from her: PS—I got the energy stuff too. Watch out, I may be on your heels! Cassie shot back a response: As if! and practically skipped to the shower.

LAURA

GETTING ORGANIZED FOR this trip was proving to be a major undertaking. First, they had a carrier installed on top of the SUV to keep the luggage. Then they had a bike rack put on the back to hold the bicycles. The amount of stuff they wanted to bring seemed ridiculous. They would be lucky if they got five miles to the gallon with this set up.

"Remind me again," she said at the dinner table. "Why are we driving to the wedding again? It's over a thousand miles. Have we lost our minds?"

"Oh pleeeaaassee, Mom," John said. "Not this after begging for a big family trip."

"Maybe to see one of the wonders of the natural world?" Sam offered.

"I know, I know," Laura admitted. "It's going to be awesome."

"It better be, I'm missing baseball camp for it," Jesse complained.

"Once we actually get on the road, it's going to be

great," Dan said. "I think it's perfect, actually. The wedding, the beach, the Grand Canyon, my sabbatical..."

"Dad," Jesse asked. "What do you actually do on your sabbatical?"

"Well, I'm expected to turn in a first draft on a textbook collaboration. But the real answer is, not much."

"Hey. Don't get too excited, some of us are actually going back to the classroom." Laura didn't like to talk about it, but she was scared shitless to start her graduate program. She had been out of that mind frame for a long time now; she was hoping she would get back into the swing of things easily. Especially with Dan able to do more at home during his sabbatical. What an awesome surprise that had been.

He had come to her as she was still in bed nursing *her* hangover from the bachelorette party. "My sabbatical was approved. I don't think the timing could be better. It's my turn to support you in your endeavors."

"That's wonderful, honey. I suppose I really have to show up for class now."

"Trust me, you're going to do great," he said with a smile, still so handsome.

Laura suspected that he wanted the break from the classroom so that he didn't have to be around the students. . . the girls. If true, she thought it was a good sign. He continued to see Phil once a week and hadn't pressured her into going. Maybe he didn't want her to, she didn't know. And she didn't really care, because today she was sitting at her table eating with her family, and no matter how tenuous it might be, today there was peace.

JOYCE

JOYCE LIKED TO print a packing list before a trip, it helped her to stay organized. Years ago, she had typed an exhaustive list of anything she might possibly bring for travel. Underwear, tampons, swimming suit, phone charger, travel snacks—it was a thorough list that she had refined with many trips. She would print the master list and then check off, or if necessary write a number next to how many to bring, all of the items needed. She had even updated her master list with the marathon specific items: the outfit chosen, the energy supplements, light sunglasses, headphones. Everything was packed in one suitcase and sitting next to the front door.

There wasn't much she needed to bring for the wedding other than a simple dress. It was to be a casual affair at the beach with Dan officiating. At Jacob and Cassie's request, he got ordained online and it was all set. Joyce was to walk with Cassie to meet Jacob in the ceremony. *Not* giving her away, Cassie insisted, (she hated the phrase), but *accompanying* her. Joyce felt ready to go as she waited for Jacob and Cassie to pick her up to go the airport.

It wasn't until she heard the horn honk outside that she realized one item that she forgot that wasn't on the list. Andy's ashes.

They were in the closet, she knew exactly where, but she didn't know where she would pack them. Her suitcase was completely full. She heard the horn honk again in impatience.

She yelled, "Shit!" to an empty house. She had a small backpack somewhere, it used to be Andy's that he took on hikes. The box should fit in that if she could find it. Maybe it was in the coat closet? She was digging through the winter coats trying to locate it when Cassie opened the door.

"Mom, what's going on? Hurry up, we need to leave."

She wanted to scream she was so pissed at herself. "Oh Cassie, I really messed up."

Her daughter's face fell. "What is it?"

She was fighting back tears. "I forgot to pack your dad's ashes. I am such a moron, I'm so sorry. I was just looking for something to put the box in, my suitcase is full. Do you think you have room in yours?"

Cassie's face softened. "Is that all? Don't worry about it, okay?"

"What do you mean don't worry about it? We had a

plan."

Cassie shrugged. "Plans change. I don't need the box to have Daddy there. Okay?"

"Are you sure?" Joyce asked.

"Yes, I'm sure," Cassie said and smiled. "Come on, let's go."

So Joyce picked up her suitcase and walked with her daughter outside to the car. And the sun was shining bright, inviting them to their day.

ABOUT THE AUTHOR

Molly Krause is the author of the memoir *Float On,* the novel *Joy Again*, and the cookbook *The Cook's Book of Intense Flavors*. Her writing has appeared in numerous publications including *Brain, Child*; *Ragazine*, and *Front Porch Review*. She lives in Lawrence, Kansas with her husband and two daughters. When not hunched over a laptop writing, walking the border collies Lucy and Desi, or chasing down her teenage daughters, attending adult ballet class is the highlight of her week.

Stay in touch with Molly at molly-krause.com.

www.ingramcontent.com/pod-product-compliance
Lightning Source LLC
Chambersburg PA
CBHW031059270626
47155CB00027B/2819